Welcome to the wonderful world of Regency Romance!
For a free short story and to listen to me read the first
chapter of all my other Regencies, please go to my website:

https://romancenovelsbyglrobinson.com

Thank you!

GL Robinson

Imogen

or

Love And Money

A Regency Romance

By

GL Robinson

As always, in memory of my
dear sister, Francine.

With thanks to my Beta Readers,
who always tell me what they think.

And with special thanks to CS
for his patient editing and technical help,
and more especially, for his friendship.

Contents

Chapter One.. 11

Chapter Two.. 15

Chapter Three.. 25

Chapter Four... 33

Chapter Five... 45

Chapter Six.. 59

Chapter Seven.. 75

Chapter Eight.. 85

Chapter Nine... 93

Chapter Ten... 105

Chapter Eleven.. 113

Chapter Twelve.. 125

Chapter Thirteen.. 137

Chapter Fourteen.. 149

Chapter Fifteen... 161

Chapter Sixteen... 169

Chapter Seventeen... 179

Chapter Eighteen.. 191

Chapter Nineteen.. 201

Chapter Twenty.. 215

Chapter Twenty-one.. 225

A Note from the Author...................................... 235

Regency Novels by GL Robinson 236

About The Author 241

Chapter One

"I heard you say quite distinctly, 'Move her out.'" The pretty young widow looked directly into his eyes without a hint of humor.

Ivo Rutherford had sighed as he walked into the foyer of the Hôtel Fleuri. It was a late evening in April, the air becoming damp as the sun set and the humidity rose from the lake. Lausanne had never been very welcoming in the spring. Lac Leman was fine and good in midsummer when the sails of small boats and the parasols of women in pretty dresses decorated its waters, but, by and large, he was beginning to wish he had never come. But, needs must. He had handed his hat and cane to the waiting liveried boy, and shrugged out of his greatcoat, letting it fall behind him with the cool assumption that it would be caught. He certainly did not look to see. He strode forward, a very tall, commanding figure, broad shouldered and with an absolute air of assurance. His entrance had been observed by a very pretty lady dressed in black.

"Bonsoir, Monsieur le Duc." The Maître d'hôtel, a short, stout man with oiled hair and a pince-nez, had come bustling from behind a shiny mahogany desk, and as he reached the visitor, he bowed, an anxious look on his face.

"Bonsoir Legrand," had come the response. "My bags are in the carriage outside. Have them brought up to my room at once."

"Mille excuses, Milor', but your accustomed chambre, she is not disponible."

"What do you mean, not available? I require it. It is my room. I am here."

"Mais non! Zat is ze problem, she is not available. A lady, a widow lady, is in occupation."

"I sent no lady, widowed or otherwise, so it is impossible one should be there, unless, of course," amended Monsieur le Duc, "you have performed this service for me. In which case I will delay my thanks until I see the lady in question." His eyes danced with amusement.

"Non, non, non!" The harassed little man, finding his English had deserted him, went into a flood of French.

The visitor listened with the light of humor still in his eyes and when the flood had run itself to a trickle, responded in an even tone, "I apprehend that a widowed lady arrived without notice, and you gave her the room that has been reserved for me these last ten summers. The solution appears obvious: move her out."

"Mais, Milor'! You 'ave nevair in ten years come before July, and now is April. You were not expected. She is installed. It is impossible to move one such as she!"

"'One such as she?' Why? What is she? The Dowager Queen? I do not wish to stand upon formality but no one else outranks me!" And, since the Maître d'hôtel appeared lost in the grades of English nobility, Milor' said it all again, in rapid French.

A clear English voice had spoken suddenly from behind them. It was the pretty lady in black. "I'm sorry to interrupt," she said, "but I believe I am the cause of all the trouble. I will gladly move into a different room."

Ivo Rutherford, Duke of Sarisbury, had turned and beheld the owner of the voice. His jaw did not drop, for he was far too well bred to allow any extreme emotion to betray him, but it is safe to say he was speechless for several seconds. The lady in front of him was indeed a widow, if her black gown, cap and gloves were any indication, but to call her the dowager anything would have been a gross injustice. She was very young, not more than her early twenties, if his Grace was any judge, and when it came to women, he was. Perhaps a little below average height, her figure was nonetheless perfect. Her black gown, high to the throat, was molded to her bosom and waist, its folds flowing over her perfect hips, flat stomach, and rounded derriere. It demonstrated the hand of an expert *modiste*. A beautiful blush glowed in her ivory skin, her wide green eyes were fringed by long black lashes and glossy curls showed enticingly around the edges of a very becoming lace cap. She had looked calmly up at him, a faint enquiry in her finely arched brows.

He immediately understood what M. Legrand had meant by "one such as she." This was not a woman one could thrust out of her bedchamber. Indeed, the bedchamber was her natural milieu. His Grace was not of a fanciful nature, but he could well imagine pages bringing her peeled grapes and bonbons on silken cushions. Doors should fly open as she approached and gravel should be smoothed before she put her foot upon it. The Duke was very far from being a romantic, in fact many of his mistresses had accused him of being cruel and hardhearted, but he felt himself springing to the defense of this vision.

"You misunderstand me, dear lady!" he had said, the smile lighting his eyes, "I meant nothing of the sort."

But she was having none of it. "As I say, I heard you. You told M. Legrand to move me out. Well, I am quite ready to be moved out. If I had known the room was reserved for someone of such elevated *rank*," she again looked him straight in the eye, ignoring the smile in them, "I would never have accepted it in the first place." She turned to M. Legrand. "If you would find me alternative accommodations, I will have my maid move my things in a trice."

"My dear Madam," Monsieur le Duc, rarely at a loss for words, was once again almost speechless. "I beg you to reconsider. I... I cannot possibly sleep peacefully in a room knowing you have been... ejected from it. Legrand should never have suggested such a thing."

But the lady was already walking away. "He did not suggest it, you did. As I say, I heard you. There is nothing to discuss. I am going for a walk and by the time I return, I expect my things to have been moved." She nodded at Legrand, "Thank you, Monsieur." She stopped and dropped a shallow curtsey. "Good evening, Your Grace." And she left.

Both men stood stock still for a moment. Legrand was the first to recover. He clapped his hands at the liveried boy and when he came forward, whispered in his ear. The boy ran off, presumably to have Madame's belongings moved. The Duke hesitated, but realizing that the situation was now out of his control, shrugged. He moved into the lounge, calling over his shoulder for a bottle of claret.

Chapter Two

The Duke settled himself in the lounge without pleasure in a high-backed armchair that was far too low for him, forcing him to sit with his knees at an uncomfortable angle. However, it allowed him to keep an unobtrusive eye on the front door. He was puzzled by the widow, whose name, he realized, he did not know. Her gown was not that of a countrywoman, but he had never met her in London. She looked like a Botticelli angel, with that ivory skin, green eyes, and copper curls, visible in spite of the widow's cap. But her demeanor was anything but angelic. She had no fear of speaking her mind or answering back a man she must know to be her social superior. Accustomed to being courted rather than smartly talked back to, he was both intrigued and not a little annoyed. He waited to give her one of his famous set-downs. But he waited in vain. The widow did not return through the front door and the Duke was at length obliged to go to the room that was now indisputably his, and change for dinner.

Entering the dining room nearly an hour later, Ivo saw her at once. She was sitting alone, reading, at a small table facing the door and did not look up as he came in. She, too, had changed for dinner and now wore a black gown with a décolleté that tantalizingly revealed the tops of her breasts. She wore no jewelry except a large gold locket, containing the hair or other memento of her late husband, he surmised. He approached her table. She looked up as he came near, and regarded him calmly with her wide green eyes. He was accustomed to a more effusive welcome from the women he chose to honor with his attention, and did not at once know how to begin. She did not help him, but waited patiently for him to say something.

"You have the advantage of me, Madam," he began. "You know my name but I do not know yours."

"You are mistaken, Your Grace," she replied. "I know only that you are a Duke. I did not hear your name."

"Then allow me to present myself. Ivo Rutherford, Duke of Sarisbury." He bowed.

"And I am Imogen Mainwaring." She acknowledged his bow with a nod, but with no change in her tone. "I am the widow of Fordyce Mainwaring. He died three months ago."

"Fordyce Mainwaring was your husband?" his Grace was astonished. "But I always thought…."

"You thought," interrupted Imogen swiftly, "that he was a confirmed bachelor. I know. But nonetheless he married me."

"He never brought you to London, or we would surely have met. I saw him there from time to time."

"That is so. I had no desire to live in London. We had a quiet life in Nottingham."

"But why are we talking like this? May I not sit? I believe we are the only two English speaking people here. It would seem natural for us to dine together." His Grace spoke, sure of the answer. But he was to be disappointed.

"I do not wish to seem inhospitable, but I am not yet good company for anyone. Please excuse me." Imogen smiled slightly and returned to the book she had been reading when he came in.

Finding himself thus dismissed, the Duke proceeded in some discomfort to another table. He had never before been refused a place at her table by a woman and he hardly knew how to act. Gradually, anger replaced his discomfiture and as he looked at her, calmly drinking her soup and eating her sole, he vowed she would change her tune and in the not too distant future.

After dinner, it was the habit of the guests in the Hôtel Fleuri to gather in the lounge for liqueurs and conversation. His Grace made his way there and reviewed the company. He had been coming here for years, but, as M. Legrand had pointed out, only in the summer. In that season the double doors that gave onto the balcony would be open, the gardens below would be lit with candles in glass lanterns, and a small orchestra would be playing, outside if weather permitted, and inside if it did not. Young men enjoying the Grand Tour would travel to Geneva and Lausanne to escape the heat of Italy and would come there to dine and dance. They attracted young women of laughing dispositions and easy virtue who were quite ready to entertain the English Milor' who spoke their language so charmingly and who was ready to pay for any extravagance.

However, in April the company was quite different. There were a couple of family groups, the stout Papa stuffed into britches that were too small and a coat that was too short, the Mama in her outmoded narrow gown and feathers, and two or three older ladies with their female companions. One of these in particular brushed deliberately close to his Grace when walking past his chair, but he did not rise to the bait. He was thinking about Imogen Mainwaring.

She, meanwhile, had decided to take a stroll outside rather than go into the lounge. In the week she had been at the hotel, she had gone there often enough after dinner to know that the company was not especially entertaining. The ladies had shaken their heads at her widow's weeds and pressed her hand, and their husbands had been ponderously polite, offering their seats and bringing her drinks she did not want. She had taken to walking around the gardens and looking down towards the lake. Her unexpected widowhood had shaken her in ways she had not been prepared for. Her relationship with her much older spouse had been based on friendship rather than passionate love, but she missed her husband more than she could have imagined. The inky black Lac Leman somehow helped to swallow up her mixed feelings.

On this night she had another reason for not staying inside. The Duke had both irritated and attracted her. She had heard his peremptory demand for "his" room, and his assertion that he outranked everyone except the Dowager Queen and had determined that he was an insufferable prig. But when he had stared at her in obvious admiration with that smile in his eyes, she had been surprised to find herself flattered, and had had to control an impulse to respond to him. It had been on the tip of her tongue to ask him to dine with her, before he declared he had known her husband and had seemed to question her marriage, and then she had not wanted to explain herself any more. But it was getting uncomfortably damp and chilly, so, wrapping herself more closely in her cloak, she walked slowly back to the hotel. She entered by the back door, so was not seen by anyone as she made her way to her room and rang for her maid.

The next morning, Imogen took her breakfast in her room, as she usually did, and did not see the Duke until luncheon. He came in after she had been seated, but apart from inclining his head as he passed her table, he did not engage with her. She felt rather let down, but merely returned nod for nod. That afternoon she took a carriage ride to the Chateau Saint-Maire. The little guide book she had been reading described it as an important historical monument in Lausanne. It had been the Bishop's residence until church property had been seized in 1536 and the bishop had been forced to escape through a hidden staircase. It was not exactly a beautiful building, especially since a modern annex had been attached about forty years previously, but the secret staircase was suitably dark and frightening. One of the Swiss couples from the hotel was on the same trip and the Papa was particularly attentive to the beautiful widow. He insisted on helping her down stairs when she would have been far better off on her own, since his girth made the passage almost impossible. But it was all done with such good humor and friendliness that she arrived back at the Hôtel Fleuri in higher spirits than she had enjoyed in weeks. These were a little dashed when she observed the Duke conversing in rapid French with an old lady and her companion, a faded blond with a raddled neck and painted eyebrows. She saw the faded blond place her hand on the Duke's arm and leave it there.

Dinner passed much the same as luncheon. The Duke came in a little after Imogen was seated but made no attempt to join her. He went instead to make his bow to the old lady and her companion and was soon seated with them. However, her Swiss protector from the afternoon, seeing her sitting alone, invited her to dine at his family table. The couple had two children: a boy of about ten and a girl a couple of years younger. They were both at first shy with the English Madame, but when she spoke to them in her schoolgirl French and acted out the scene in the stairwell that afternoon, they were soon laughing and talking as if they had known her all their life. His Grace saw her gaiety with the Swiss family and decided that his tactics were not working. This called for a less subtle approach.

It had come on to drizzle in the late afternoon, so walking in the gardens was not possible that evening. Needing a breath of fresh air, Imogen opened one of the tall windows onto the balcony and was immediately met with a chorus of complaints from the Swiss guests about the noxious quality of the night air and the inadvisability of letting in a draught. So she stepped outside and drew the door closed behind her. The lounge terrace had the bedroom balconies above it and was thus sheltered from the rain. She had only been there a few minutes when the door opened and his Grace stepped out. He seemed surprised to see her there, though in reality he had seen her open the windows and go outside.

"Mrs. Mainwaring! I did not know you were there! I had thought to smoke a cigar before going up, but I do not want to discommode you." He made as if to leave.

"Oh, no," cried Imogen, before thinking, "I like the smell of a cigar. It reminds me of… of my husband. He used to enjoy one after dinner."

"In the… confusion over our accommodations, I don't think I expressed my condolences yesterday." The Duke bowed towards her. "I'm sorry to hear of Fordy Mainwaring's death. He was not exactly a friend, but I knew him as a kind and affable fellow. Had he been ill for long?"

"No, his death was... unexpected. He suffered from an apoplexy. While visiting... a friend."

"Then it must have been doubly painful for you. I'm sorry. I've never been married myself and I can't imagine how you must feel, losing your husband while you are still so young."

Wanting to change the subject, Imogen muttered something and moved towards the stone balustrade overlooking the gardens. She placed her hands on the rounded edge and leaned forward. The Duke was shocked to see a large piece of stone under her right-hand wobble and then become dislodged, falling with a crash to the ground. With a cry of distress, she teetered for a moment, her right arm waving as she tried to catch her balance. Flinging the cigar from his hand, his Grace took three rapid strides with his long legs and caught her around the waist. She clung to him, her heart pounding, as he drew her back towards the building. They stood like that for a few moments, she breathless, he enjoying the sensation of holding this lovely creature in his arms and thanking the gods for loose stonework.

Finally, Imogen looked up at him and said, "I think you can let go of me now. I'm sorry. The falling stone shocked me. I don't think I would actually have tumbled over the edge, but it gave me a fright."

The Duke threw caution to the winds. "Since it gave me the opportunity to do something I have wanted to do since I first saw you, I can only be grateful for it. And I think you suffered a greater shock than you say. I can still feel your heart pounding."

Imogen did not know what to say. His words, lacking in propriety as they were, and spoken in a tone that was both caressing and suggestive, brought a slight gasp to her throat. It was true her heart was pounding, but now more from the effect of being held by two very strong arms against a broad muscled chest, than from the fear of falling.

"We should make sure there was no one underneath to be injured by the falling stone, but I think not, in this miserable rain. And I must inform Legrand his balustrade needs repair, but not quite yet, I think." His grip around her did not lessen. In the darkness she could not see his face, but there was a smile in his voice. "Come, Mrs. Mainwaring, I think we have some bridges to mend. I fear the circumstances of our meeting set us off on the wrong foot. Let us begin again. I am Ivo Rutherford, you are Imogen Mainwaring. We are two English people together in a foreign country. Let us be friends, if only for the duration of our stay. Pretending not to notice each other is foolish. What do you say?"

Imogen looked up at him again. "You are right, of course. We have both behaved like children. I am prepared to be your friend, I suppose, so long," she hesitated, "so long as you behave with propriety. But first, you must release me. We cannot stand out here like this any longer or the other guests will have a completely different notion of our... friendship. Let me go, please."

"I find propriety vastly overrated," replied his Grace. "It usually prevents one doing what one wants to do. But I notice you did not ask me to let you go because you dislike my holding you. Dare I entertain hopes?"

"No, you may not," retorted Imogen. "I am but recently a widow and anyway...," she thought how to end her sentence. "Anyway, I am not interested in... that," she ended lamely.

"Pity. Friendship let it be, then." The Duke dropped his arms and stood away from her. He walked swiftly back to where the stone had fallen and leaned over. There was no one underneath. He came back. "No prone body on the ground, so that excitement is spared us. Now, let us go in. You hold onto my arm looking as if you are about to faint and I shall complain loudly about broken balustrades. That will quiet any wagging tongues."

"But I never faint," protested Imogen.

"They don't know that. Come on!" He led her into the lounge.

Chapter Three

As Imogen did not come down for breakfast and the Duke himself had a morning engagement in a fencing school in town, the two did not meet again until luncheon. He quietly told M. Legrand that he and Mrs. Mainwaring would be lunching and dining together from now on and she should be shown to his table, which was much larger.

When she commented upon this, he replied airily, "Oh they know to give me a larger space. I'm too big to sit at one of those enlarged saucers they call dinner tables here. I am forever knocking the bread onto the floor and my wine into my soup."

"But you alone are taking up as much space as a family of four!" protested his companion.

"If I were a marrying man, which I most decidedly am not," he replied, "I could easily take up a table like this with my family, so I don't see why I shouldn't have one just because I have decided not to marry. Anyway, now that you are here, I am no longer alone - though you don't take up much space at all. You may sit comfortably in that corner while I spread myself everywhere else."

"How kind!" she retorted. "What if I wish to spread myself?"

He grinned engagingly. "I wish I may see how you achieve that! I'm sure you fit very nicely into any armchair, carriage, bathtub, or bed, all of which I have to have specially made for me. I assure you; the life of a tall man is anything but easy! I have to sit with my knees under my chin or try to fold myself in half most of the time. Why are you laughing? I should be an object of your pity, not amusement!"

He tried to look downcast, but only made her laugh all the more. Her merriment caught the attention of the faded blond companion, who looked sourly at her, and of the stout gentleman from the day before, who lifted his glass and smiled in her direction.

"I suppose that is true," she said at last. "I've never thought of it before, but I can see it must be very inconvenient. How do you find the furniture here in Switzerland? Does it fit you?"

"Mostly, yes, because they are inclined to corpulence, like your friend over there. The chairs are too low, but at least they are wide enough. But perhaps you were referring to my bed? Or should I say *your* bed; it was yours before it was mine. Though as a matter of fact, the reason why I insist upon that bedchamber is because it has the longest bed in the place. Should you like me to lie on it to demonstrate? I am quite willing to do so, if you would lie beside me, purely for the sake of comparison, of course."

Imogen blushed. "I was referring to nothing of the sort, Your Grace, which you very well know! If you continue in this inappropriate way, I shall ask to be moved back to my own table!"

The Duke raised his hands in mock horror. "I was only answering in full your most kind enquiry. I pray you not to desert me for so innocent an error! And am I to be 'Your Grace' at every tiff and turn? Please tell me that I may call you Imogen and you will call me Ivo."

"Nothing you say can ever be deemed innocent! And it seems most improper to use Christian names when we have known each other for only two days. I don't think I could."

"Well, I can and will call you Imogen. You may call me what you please. You would be amazed at the names I've been called in my life, mostly by women."

"On the contrary, I am not at all amazed. You are the most infuriating person! Very well, I shall call you Ivo while we are here. But if I ever meet you anywhere else…."

"You can pretend not to know me at all," completed the Duke. "I shall understand."

Luckily, the fish arrived before Imogen was required to make a response to this, and they both began to eat. The Duke was pleased to note that his companion ate heartily, and did not merely pick at her food, like so many women of his acquaintance. He had observed in his quite extensive study of the opposite sex that women who enjoyed eating also enjoyed the other sensual pleasures. However, she refused the wine he offered her, saying that drinking wine in the afternoon made her sleepy. Since the prospect of a slightly drowsy Imogen was what he had been looking forward to, he was disappointed. Instead, she brightly remarked that she hoped he would not mind if she consulted her guide book, to see where she might go that afternoon. It had become her habit, she said, to take in the local sights after luncheon.

"But my dear Imogen, you have no need of guide books," said his Grace. "I have been coming here every summer since my Grand Tour after leaving Oxford. I had an idea to visit Geneva, but

I found it unbearably puritanical. Calvin was their most famous citizen, as I expect you know. So I fled to Lausanne, which wasn't much better, but I finally found myself here. I liked its pleasant outlook and the food has always been surprisingly good, so I stayed. I formed the habit of coming here in the summer when London is so stifling. *Enfin, bref,*" his Grace became decidedly continental, "I know the place very well and can take you to all the interesting spots. There aren't many."

"I visited the Chateau Saint-Maire yesterday," said Imogen. "I got stuck in the secret stairway with M. Charpentier, over there," She indicated the stout gentleman. "It was quite funny, really. He thought he was helping me, but there simply wasn't space for both of us."

"I'm sorry to have missed it, I would have offered my services and made sure you became stuck with me." His eyes danced with amusement.

"Don't be ridiculous," responded Imogen tartly, totally ignoring his suggestive expression. "Anyway, I don't think you could have bent your head low enough to even enter the stairway. It was quite low and dark."

"Low and dark! Better and better! I would have fallen to my knees if it had meant I could have been stuck in the dark with you. Are you sure you don't want to revisit the place today so we can try it?"

"Definitely not! Stop looking at me like that! Let us change the subject. Why are you here in April instead of July this year?"

The answer was delayed as the waiter arrived with the meat course and the Duke ordered a bottle of burgundy to go with it. There was a lengthy pause as the sommelier went through the process of cork extraction, sniffing, decanting, and pouring so that his Grace could taste it.

The Duke took a mouthful of the wine and appearing to find it satisfactory, he nodded dismissal to the sommelier and asked, "Now, what were we talking about?"

"Don't prevaricate," answered Imogen smartly. "You know very well what we were talking about. I asked you why you are here."

"Gracious! What a schoolmarm you are! Have you no delicacy? Perhaps this is a sensitive subject I prefer not to discuss and am trying subtly to avoid."

"If that is so, you have only to say. I have no desire to hear any confidences, I simply want to move the conversation away from your salacious innuendo."

"I am dismayed by your description of my conversation! Salacious innuendo indeed! I speak with the tongue of an innocent! But I see that I shall have to lay the sad facts before you. I am running from English Justice. I killed a man in a duel."

"Now you are funning with me. Very well, if you do not wish to tell me, don't! We can talk about something else."

"What a sorry state we are in, when a man cannot tell a lady the truth and have her believe him! I assure you; it is the unvarnished truth. I killed a man. It was unintended: I meant only to give him the merest graze, but the silly fool, in an act of what I suppose was overweening courage, ran forward, tripped, and fell on my sword. He expired on the spot, and rather than face the inevitable wrangling about who was to blame for the unfortunate ending of an event that should never have taken place at all, I decided to leave the country."

Imogen sat stock still, a look of horror on her face. "But… but, dueling is against the law! And if you ran away it must make it seem you are to blame for the poor man's death, and… and anyway, why on earth were you dueling at all, and with swords? It's like an Elizabethan drama!"

"Of course, you are right in everything you say. It is against the law, and if the idiot had just let me pink him, no one would have been any the wiser. The doctor would have bound him up and we might even have gone to the pub for breakfast together. That's what usually happens."

"Usually!" gasped Imogen. "You mean this has happened before?"

"Naturally! When a man finds out another man has been… friends with his wife, a duel is almost inevitable. I always chose swords because they are less dangerous than pistols. I'm an excellent fencer, everyone knows it, and I can always just pink my opponent in the arm, spill a spoonful of his blood, and it's over. But this unlucky fellow must have thought I chose swords in order to kill him, why on earth, I don't know. Why should I kill a man over a woman I was already tired of? Anyway, he ran at me in the most foolhardy manner. I had no time to avoid him. On the other hand, the way he was running at me, if I had not stopped him, I would have been the one lying on the grass, so perhaps it is just as well. I simply could not be bothered to stay for all the explanations, so here I am."

The Duke took a long, reflective swallow of his burgundy while Imogen just stared at him. She was speechless. Not living in London, she was unaware of the relaxed morals that pertained among the upper classes of society. It was not at all uncommon for a bored wife to seek amusement elsewhere, and neither were duels uncommon, although they were illegal. As his Grace had said, in the general way, there was no real intent of serious injury. It was a matter of satisfaction being sought and received, after which the antagonists were often quite cordial with each other. But Imogen was staggered. That her luncheon companion should have been engaged in a duel was amazing enough. That he should have been involved in several was almost beyond belief. And he had already been tired of the lady! How many ladies were there, she wondered? But of course, that was a question she could not ask.

"Returning to the question of what one might visit this afternoon," said his Grace, ignoring the fact that Imogen was still at a loss for words, "might I suggest we go into the town and take a look at the cathedral? It's thirteenth century."

Shaken out of her wonderment at her companion's easy acceptance of infidelity, dueling and even death, Imogen nodded. "Yes... yes, that sounds very interesting. Should we ask M. Legrand to hire us a carriage?"

"Not at all. I have my own. I told you, I dislike sitting with my knees under my chin, so whenever I can I bring my own vehicle."

"What an extravagance!" thought Imogen, but aloud she said, "How convenient. But if we are to visit the Cathedral, you will excuse me, I must change, so I shall go up now. I take no sweet course. Let us meet in the lounge in, say, an hour." She stood up from the table, gathering her reticule and guide book. As the Duke made to rise, she said, "Please don't get up! We are friends, are we not? No need to stand on ceremony."

"As well tell the sun not to rise," commented the Duke, "as tell me not to get up when a lady leaves my presence. Bred in the bone, I'm afraid." He smiled and bowed.

She smiled back and left the room, waving to the stout gentleman and his family, who were still enjoying their copious repast.

Chapter Four

It was a little more than an hour later when she found her new friend in the lounge. He had obviously been drinking coffee with the old lady and the faded blond. They were all laughing at something when she walked in. The Duke leaped to his feet and looked at her appreciatively. She had changed from her silk day dress into a fine woolen walking outfit in the inevitable black. It had a full skirt, cut close into the waist and topped with a very fitted jacket. This featured a peplum that enhanced the narrowness of her waist, while the close fit of the top was molded to her bosom. A white silk blouse with ruffles peeped out around her throat and wrists. A large braided hair brooch, almost certainly a memento of her late husband, sat at her throat in the center of her ruffled collar. She wore a black felt hat with a brim, not too large, turned up on one side, with a black feather curled towards the back. Her hair was gathered into the nape of her neck, but curling tendrils were already beginning to escape. Black kid booties and gloves completed the ensemble. Provincial woman she might be, but there was no mistaking the hand of a fashionable *modiste* in her obviously expensive apparel. The faded blond sniffed and looked away as the Duke bowed over the old lady's hand and turned towards Imogen. He shrugged on his caped greatcoat then picked up his tall hat and cane.

"I am a lucky man," he said, taking her hand. "To accompany me on a dismal afternoon to an even more dismal cathedral I have the loveliest woman in Switzerland. I have no need of the sun. Your beauty outshines any heavenly light."

"Oh, for heaven's sake," said Imogen prosaically, "all I did was change my dress."

This was, of course, an untruth, as, for reasons that she could not admit even to herself, she wanted to look her best and had spent a good deal of time deciding what to wear. She knew she looked very nice indeed, but she refused to flutter her eyelashes and simper when this man—this *rake* - chose to flatter her. She picked up her cloak.

The rake chuckled and his eyes danced. He put her arm on top of his and patted her hand. "Yes, I can see that. It's quite obvious!"

He led her outside to the waiting carriage. The doors of the shiny black exterior were emblazoned with a coat of arms showing a shield striped in gold and purple held on either side by two-headed gold eagles, with the words *Erimus Semper* above.

"It must be hard for you to travel incognito with that on your carriage," remarked Imogen.

"Why should I want to travel incognito? I find that the greater the consequence, the better the service."

"But weren't you afraid someone would see you fleeing the country?"

"When I said I fled, I was talking about rapidity not secrecy. I certainly did not skulk out of the country. When you look as I do, skulking is out of the question in any case."

He lowered the steps and helped her up into the carriage, then went to the other side and, having given instructions to the driver, climbed in himself. Imogen laughed as she sat on the seat and realized that her feet did not touch the floor. She swung them like a child.

"I see what you mean about having the carriage built for yourself. I feel about ten years old!"

"Excuse me," said the Duke, "I am not trying to touch your petticoats, though the idea is very tempting." He bent down to her ankles and pulled a step from under Imogen's seat. She put her feet on it. "There, now you may sit like a grown-up."

He sat on the other side of the carriage, and in that confined space, wearing his caped greatcoat and tall hat, he looked even larger. In spite of his arrogance and his constant attempts to discountenance her, Imogen thought he was the most attractive man she had ever met. His expressive dark eyes danced with humor more often than not under mobile brows. He had a large straight nose and a mouth that could move quickly from a stern straight line to an engaging grin. He was not classically handsome, he was far more interesting than that. He looked at her now and his eyes twinkled.

"You really are delightfully pretty, you know. I'm beginning to be glad I came to Lausanne. When I arrived the other day, it was so gloomy I nearly turned around and went back, even if they clapped me in irons."

"You are the most ridiculous man! It's impossible to believe one word in ten of what you say."

"How can you say so? I have never told you anything but the purest truth! My life is an open book. You, however, are a mystery. You haven't told me why *you* are here. It's not a destination for many English people, and certainly not widows. That, I might say, is one of its chief attractions for me. I'm surprised you even knew of its existence."

"I didn't. I didn't care for the... company in Geneva and someone suggested Lausanne and the Hôtel Fleuri. I wanted to get away from England after... after my husband's death, and I thought that Switzerland might be safe. I mean, one never hears of a Swiss Casanova! I most certainly did not want the attention of men."

"Oh dear, shall I leave the carriage?"

"Not you! I didn't mean you!"

"You mean I don't count as a man? I cannot let that go unchallenged! Only yesterday, using my immense strength, did I not save you from certain death in preventing your fall from the balcony?"

Imogen laughed. "Of course! You were heroic! I owe my life to you!"

"I'm glad you admit it! Anyway, here we are at the Cathedral. Do we really have to go in?"

"It may be better if *you* not go in, as great a sinner as you are, the angels may weep tears of stone."

"How you misrepresent me! How can I be deemed a sinner when I have led a life innocently trying to bring pleasure to others, especially women? I shouldn't be surprised if after my death they erect a statue in my honor."

Leaving his tall hat on his seat, he descended from the carriage without use of the steps then walked around to open her door and let down the steps on her side. He handed her down and walked with her into the Cathedral of Notre Dame de Lausanne. It was an odd, lopsided building, with a tower on the one side only, but inside, considering the gloominess of the April day, the white stone arches and vaulted ceiling gave the nave a lovely luminosity. It was almost totally bare, with rows of plain wooden chairs and a white altar, behind which a beautiful rose window and three arched stained-glass windows bathed the chancel in an almost golden light. They were the only people there and their footsteps rang on the stone floor.

"Apparently there used to be paintings on the walls, presumably the lives of the saints," said the Duke. "They would have been interesting, if only to give us a glimpse of life three hundred years ago. But they were covered over during the Protestant Reformation in the 1500's. It seems the Calvinists from Geneva didn't appreciate them. No wonder neither of us cares for Geneva."

They had stood still and it was very quiet inside the immense edifice. "We can't hear it from the hotel," continued the Duke, "but there is actually a watchman every night in the bell tower who calls out the hour between 10 o'clock and 2 o'clock in the morning. He does it in all four directions—north, south, east, and west. In my innocent youth I used to gather with friends underneath and shout back at him, but he never took any notice. We tried smuggling a woman of a certain reputation up there once, to see if she could make him forget to do it, but, alas, the door to the tower was locked inside. We still had to pay her, as I remember. But I think another of the group took advantage of the… free offering, I suppose you might call it." He reminisced a moment. "I know it wasn't me."

"From what I can tell, that must be the only time a woman has escaped you," remarked Imogen. "That must be why you remember it. Rather like the angler who always remembers the enormous fish he did not catch."

"I cannot imagine why you have formed this unwholesome picture of me," complained his Grace. "I keep telling you I have led a blameless existence, dedicated only to pleasing others. In fact, were they to repaint the lives of the saints on the walls here, they would put in an image of me."

Imogen laughed, both at the idea and at his Grace's affronted expression.

"I see I cannot convince you. I assure you, my adventures are always with very willing ladies of... experience, let us call it. Either married or widowed." He looked at her meaningfully. "I am not in the business of seducing innocent maidens!" He started towards a door set in the side wall. "Very well, let's go up the famous tower and shout the time from the top in all directions. It's always fun to startle the unsuspecting persons below."

Imogen laughed again and allowed herself to be led to a small arched wooden door in the left wall.

Faced with a spiraling stone stair with narrow steps, Imogen said, "You go first. I don't want you behind me staring at my...," she blushed, but luckily it was too gloomy to see her face clearly.

"What a pity," said his Grace, "I was hoping precisely to ascend with your lovely... in front of me, but I long ago learned to bear disappointment. It is to that that I ascribe my sunny disposition."

He started up the stairs with Imogen close behind. They ascended mostly in silence, except for the once or twice when the Duke muttered an oath as he knocked his head against a particularly low-lying overhead stone. Once they had completed a full spiral it was almost totally dark and Imogen felt quite alarmed. But the solid form in front of her was reassuring enough and presently they reached a sort of small landing, where narrow openings allowed the faint light of day to provide some illumination.

"It's very dark. I'm not sure I like it," said Imogen. "I'm not normally timorous, but I find it quite frightening."

"I'm sorry, I should have thought to bring a lantern," said the Duke. "Do you want to go down? Or shall I carry you the rest of the way?"

"Certainly not! I have managed this far and I shall manage the rest. Go on!"

They accomplished the rest of the steps to the accompaniment of his Grace whistling the tune of *Where Have You Been All The Day, Billy Boy* until he got to the chorus, which he sang with great gusto in a tuneful baritone:

> *And did Nancy tickle your fancy?*
> *O me charmin' Billy boy.*

This made Imogen smile and forget her fears, and before long they were at the top. The view was spectacular. One could walk around the whole tower and look over the rooftops of the town towards the Alps, down the lake towards Geneva and across the water to France. Even on a grey April afternoon it was a lovely sight.

"Oh, I'm so glad we came," cried Imogen. "Thank you so much! I never would have come up here on my own, and I honestly don't think that my stout friend M. Charpentier could fit up the stairway!"

Before she could say anything else, she was astonished to hear the Duke bellow, "C'est le guet, il a sonné trois!" He walked around the tower and repeated it three more times.

"What are you saying?" She laughed. "I understand the bit about *sonner*. That means *ring*, but the rest?"

"It means: *I am the watch. It has struck* or *rung*, if you prefer, *three*. It's how the watch shouts the hours at night. It is three o'clock, you know. If you want to be back in time for coffee and those delicious pastries, we'd better go down. I shall go ahead of you, and if you are frightened at any time, you may clutch me around the neck. I wish you would, in fact."

He started back down the stone steps and they were soon once more in almost total darkness.

"Shall I sing another song?"

The Duke had scarcely spoken the words when Imogen lost her footing and, with a cry, tumbled forwards. Reflexively, she clutched at him as she encountered his broad back and her arms went around his neck. Her face brushed against the back of his head. In a moment he had turned, his wide shoulders scraping the stone stairwell on either side, and gathered her to him. She re-found her footing a step or two higher than he, so their faces were at the same level. There in the dark, his lips met hers. She had stiffened against his embrace, but as he did not move away, and as it was very comforting to be held by two strong arms, she melted into him as he kissed her. As the tip of his tongue pushed firmly against her lips and just into her mouth, she felt a surge from her groin to her chest. At last, realizing what she was doing, Imogen broke away from him and held him away from her, her hands flat on his chest.

"Wh... what are you *doing*?" She gasped.

"I should have thought it was obvious. I was kissing you. May I do it again?"

"No! No you may not! You shouldn't have done it the first time!"

"But when a woman flings herself at me, that is usually what she wants."

"I didn't fling myself at you! I tripped! You know I did!"

"My dear Imogen, women are forever tripping into me, slipping in front of me, fainting into my arms, trailing their shawls for me to pick up, leaving their gloves in my carriage and I don't know how many other subterfuges, all with the intent of getting me to kiss them, or more likely, to marry them. But as I told you, I'm not a marrying man. I'm sorry if I misinterpreted your advance."

"It wasn't an advance! I *tripped*! You *know* I tripped!" Imogen was almost tearful with frustration. Then she took a deep breath, put her hand to her head to right her bonnet, which she felt had been knocked askew by the fall and the kiss, and said in a firm voice, "Please continue downstairs. I am quite all right. I have recovered my balance and I want nothing more than to be out of this...." She was going to say 'awful place' but thought that was unfair, since the trip to the top of the tower had been delightful, except for *this*. "Out of this darkness," she concluded.

The Duke turned and continued slowly down the steps. When they reached the little landing, he turned to look at her.

"It wasn't really so bad, was it?" he asked with a chuckle. But he was surprised at the anger in her answer.

"Yes, it was. Very bad. I'm surprised at you and ashamed of myself. If I ever gave you reason to think I would welcome your advances, I'm sorry. You may be sure I am not one of those women you describe, dropping her shawl, losing her gloves, pretending to faint. I have never been like that and I never shall be. Please take me back to the hotel and we shall never mention it again. I think our friendship must be at an end."

Ivo was astonished. Of course, he knew she had tripped, and he did not really think she was trying to make him kiss her. But the vehemence of her response was completely unexpected. It was true that women were constantly trying to ensnare him. He knew himself to be a man of considerable address and his fortune was large. He had been the chief prize on the marriage market for years and his success with women was legendary. He had merely taken this opportunity to kiss a lovely woman who had, quite literally, fallen into his arms. He had meant nothing by it, or almost nothing. In any other circumstances and with any other woman it would have been laughed off, or even if it had been followed by a more intimate encounter, neither party would have taken it seriously. But here was this lovely creature, so open and charming in her demeanor, so obviously made for love, but who was clearly affronted by his casual embrace. And, he thought, as he continued silently down the stairs, the devil of it was, he would have sworn, as he kissed her, that she had never been kissed like that before. Yet she had been a married woman. Here was a mystery.

They reached the bottom of the stairs. The Duke held open the old wooden door into the nave and Imogen stalked through it. She walked straight through the Cathedral and out to the carriage without a word. He put down the step for her, and when he tried to take her arm to help her up, she shook him off and mounted the steps by herself. She settled herself and looked steadfastly out of the window as they drove back to the Hôtel

Fleuri. At one point, the Duke leaned forward and began, "Imogen, please listen to me…."

She cut him off. "There is nothing for you to say or for me to listen to."

The Duke had never had to deal with a woman who so totally rebuffed him. He tried again. "But Imogen, there is no need for such an extreme reaction. I am truly sorry if I offended you. It was the instinctive response of a man to a beautiful woman who fell into his arms. Can't you accept it as a tribute rather than an insult?"

"From another man I might, but from you, with all your vaunted experience of women, I find it impossible to believe you would do anything without clear deliberation."

Since this was a very accurate observation, the Duke finally gave up.

"All right, Imogen, I admit it. I've wanted to kiss you since I met you and I took the opportunity when you tripped. I'm sorry. I promise I won't do it again. Please can we put it behind us."

Imogen looked at him. His eyes were perfectly serious.

"Very well," she said, "If you really promise. And no more remarks of an improper nature. We will be *friends*, nothing else!"

The Duke leaned forward. "If that is what you wish," he said gravely, "so be it." He held out his hand.

Imogen took it and gave a brief smile. "Thank you, Your Grace."

They drove almost in silence back to the hotel, both of them thinking over her reaction to his kiss, but for different reasons.

Chapter Five

Over the next two weeks the Duke was as good as his word. He and Imogen Mainwaring ate luncheon and dinner together, walked the town together and visited the market at the foot of the Cathedral. They descended together the Escalier du Marché, a long covered wooden stairway leading from the foot of the Cathedral into the lower part of the city. They strolled around the parks and gardens. He never treated her with anything but the utmost politeness, never referred to his scurrilous escapades and, apart from handing her in and out of his carriage, never laid a finger upon her. He talked interestingly and without insinuation. He told her the history of the region. He talked about how when the Romans retreated, the inhabitants had moved up to the top of the hill, where Lausanne was now situated; how it became a refuge for French Huguenots. Why then, when she had exactly what she had asked for, did she miss the humorously suggestive conversation of the first days of their acquaintance? Why did she miss the twinkle in his eye?

If Mrs. Mainwaring had some regrets, his Grace had none. His punctilious, humorless behavior would have surprised those who knew him well, but if it was the price he had to pay for furthering his acquaintance with the delicious widow, he was prepared to pay it. He had in no wise given up his objective of fixing her affections. He knew she had been titillated by his conversation the first days and that his recent strictly correct behavior was becoming tedious.

On a day that dawned clear and bright, with the first real sunshine of the spring, after luncheon the Duke suggested taking Mrs. Mainwaring for a row on the lake. She readily agreed, though she had had no experience at all of boats. She wore a silk dress, still in black, but with a wide white lace collar, a black straw bonnet with a wide brim, and she carried a ruffle-edged black parasol. For his part, the Duke wore a pair of white trousers with a black cutaway jacket, dark waistcoat, and a straw boater.

They took a boat kept tied up to the jetty at the bottom of the hotel gardens. For a man of his size, he climbed nimbly into the vessel and, standing firmly in the center, put strong arms around her waist to lift her down into it. The rocking alarmed Imogen and he held on to her firmly until it stopped. As before, she was conscious of his strength and his closeness. She had to force herself to breathe normally as the masculine scent of him reached her nostrils. She hoped he would ascribe her breathlessness to her fears of the instability beneath her feet rather than to him. As the day was warm, he begged to remove his jacket and unbutton his waistcoat, and he rowed with his shirt sleeves rolled up. Seeing his broad shoulders, the muscles working beneath his shirt, and his strong forearms shadowed with black hair, Imogen felt her heart beat quicken again and her throat went dry.

After about twenty minutes, he guided the boat under the fronds of a willow that reached almost to the water and tied it up to the trunk. He produced a basket from the bottom of the boat. He must have placed it there before she arrived. Within were two champagne glasses and a dish of petits fours. The champagne itself had been tethered to the boat in the water and was deliciously cool. They drank champagne and nibbled on the sweets in a private world, as the willow branches shifted in the slight breeze and the sparkling surface of the lake revealed itself in snatches between the constantly moving green curtain. Imogen felt herself relax slightly as she lay back on the cushions and looked up into the verdant canopy with the blue sky beyond. She had never been anywhere more beautiful.

The Duke had been in this spot before with a number of different women over the years. The effects of the champagne and the secluded green watery bower had never failed to produce a satisfactory result. This time, however, he maintained his polite distance, talked lightly of this and that, and refilled Imogen's glass with an air of detachment. Her senses heightened by the masculinity of his presence, she did not know whether to be grateful or disappointed. The minutes lengthened into an hour and more. Suddenly, Imogen started up, aware that, drowsy from the champagne and the rocking of the boat, she had all but fallen asleep. She sat up, self-consciously straightening her gown and her bonnet, and gave an embarrassed little laugh.

"My goodness, how rude of me! Did I fall asleep while you were talking? I do hope not!"

"The good thing about being with friends," replied his Grace gravely, "is that one need not be afraid of hurting their feelings. In this case, I'm delighted you feel so comfortable in my presence that you can nod off."

So comfortable in my presence hardly described Imogen's sensations. He had removed his boater and undone a couple of buttons at the top of his shirt. Seeing him there, lounging in the bottom of the boat with his head back on a cushion, his unbuttoned shirt revealing a glimpse of the dark hair of his chest, his strong, bare forearms, his long legs stretched out towards her, she felt his almost irresistible pull. All her earlier emotions came rushing back and she had to grip the edges of her bench to force herself to sit still. In spite of his impeccable behavior over the last two weeks, she knew instinctively that he had not brought her here in innocence. He was only too aware of his animal magnetism and was counting on her weakness to achieve his goal. Well, she gritted her teeth. She was having none of it.

She sat up straighter and said briskly, "It is getting late. We had better go back. Once the sun begins to sink it will get chilly and I don't want either of us to catch cold."

The prosaic nature of this remark was ludicrous, considering the idyllic situation, the sparkling lake, the blue sky, the warm sun, and the shifting green canopy, but neither of them laughed. The Duke merely righted himself, untied the boat, resumed his rowing position on the center bench, found his boater and guided them out into the waters of the lake. He had not re-buttoned the neck of his shirt and Imogen found it hard to keep her eyes from the glimpses of dark hair on his chest as his muscles worked the oars. The return took longer than their trip down the lake, as the current was against them. They sat in silence for over half an hour, the tension between them palpable.

When they arrived at the jetty, the Duke swiftly leaped ashore and tied up the boat, fastening the painters at both ends. He held out his hands to Imogen and took her firmly by the forearms as she stepped up onto the jetty. She stood on the wooden planks, trembling slightly, still feeling as if she were rocking.

"Thank you, Ivo," she said when she could speak evenly, "I've never been in a boat before. It was delightful. I hope you won't mind if I go to my room immediately. I think I may have had a little too much sun."

She felt she had to get away from this man before she did something foolish. She longed to leave him so she could master her emotions and yet she felt irresistibly drawn to him. She could still feel the pressure on her forearms where he had helped her out of the boat, and his scent was in her nostrils. She almost ran up the gravel of the garden path, into the blessed cool of the hotel and up to her room. She threw off her bonnet and gown and lay on the bed in her petticoat, her chest heaving.

Some half an hour later, when her breathing had returned more or less to normal, she rang for her maid and instructed her to bring tea. She had had too much sun, she said, and would not be going down for dinner. A bowl of soup in her room later on would suffice. Having picked up her garments from the floor, her maid curtseyed and went to fetch the tea. It took some while and several cups of tea before Imogen completely calmed down.

Then she fell into a doze and when she awoke it was dark outside. She went to the windows and opened them, looking out at the inky surface of the lake with its ripples embroidered here and there by the white light of a fitful moon. The air was cool now, and she breathed in huge gulps of it. In due course, the soup arrived and although she did not feel like eating, she forced it down. Her maid helped her prepare to retire for the night, putting on her nightgown and wrapper, taking the pins from her hair and brushing out her curls. She sat down in an armchair by the bed, her unopened guide book in her lap, wondering what to do about Ivo Rutherford, Duke of Sarisbury.

For his part, after Imogen had left so precipitously, the Duke smiled wryly to himself as he buttoned his waistcoat, donned his jacket, and gathered up the basket, the empty bottle and glasses, and, perceiving it lying in the bottom of the boat, Imogen's parasol. He walked slowly up to the hotel where he deposited all of his burden except the parasol on M. Legrand's desk. He wandered into the lounge, carrying the rolled-up parasol, not really expecting to see Imogen there, and fell into conversation with the old lady and the faded blond companion. He explained the origins of the parasol and the afternoon excursion on the lake. The faded blond sniffed and said nothing, but the old lady recalled boat trips of her youth and was pleased to reminisce about the manners and customs pertaining to the last quarter of the previous century.

No single woman, widow or otherwise, it seemed, would have ventured out in a boat alone with a man when she was a girl. What would her dear Mama say if she were to see the freedom of women today? She shuddered to think. She had not been allowed to be alone even with her fiancé. Her mother had been most strict on that point. A duenna had accompanied her everywhere. Of course, she and her dear Frederik, dead now these twenty years, alas, still found ways of communicating privately. He would drop his handkerchief and under cover of picking it up, slide a note under her shoe. Ah! How happy they had been! Her voice dithered off into silence, and the three of them sat for a while in quiet contemplation, she remembering stolen kisses and surreptitiously pressed palms, he thinking how uncomfortably frustrated poor Frederik must have been, and her faded companion thinking that there would be nothing surreptitious in her dealings with a man, especially this one.

At length, the old lady murmured something about changing for dinner. This somewhat surprised the Duke as he had rather thought her clothing all to be the same: dusty black, with a multiplicity of folds, capes, and shawls, so that one garment was indistinguishable from another. It is true that this afternoon she wore a very fine necklace of jet around what was at one time her neck, together with matching pendants in her overlarge earlobes. Perhaps it was these that she changed. The Duke resolved to look more closely when he saw her later. He stood and bowed as the ladies made their slow way out of the lounge, and then took himself upstairs on the same errand, carrying with him the black parasol.

Returning about an hour later after a bath and complete change of clothes, he now wore a pair of narrow grey trousers, finely striped, with a long, waisted black jacket in superfine wool. His tall, snow-white collar enclosed a wide cravat in complicated folds. The prevailing style in menswear was for padded shoulders and puffed sleeves, but these his Grace distained, his own shoulders already being very broad and his arms extremely muscular from almost daily fencing practice. He also disdained the very tightly waisted frock coat requiring a corset, worn by dandies in London and Paris, laughing to his tailor that the only corset he was prepared to remove would be on a woman, not himself.

He came into the lounge, still carrying the parasol, intending to return it to its owner. She was not there and he waited in vain for her appearance. The old lady and her companion did come down at last and he was able to examine the older woman's garments. He could perceive no difference in them at all but he did see that she had changed her jet beads for black pearls. These, the Duke knew, were extremely rare and expensive and he briefly wondered whether he might be able to persuade her to sell them—since everyone on the Continent knew Englishmen were unaccountable, such an offer would not be too surprising -

so that he might offer them to Imogen. He commented on them flatteringly and was told they had been bought twenty years before in honor of her dear Frederik, so he abandoned that idea. He waited until everyone else had gone in for dinner and at length decided that Imogen was not coming. Not a little annoyed, he ate a solitary dinner, resolving to bring things to a head with her that very night.

Imogen had just settled into the chair by her bed, and her maid was putting away the last of her clothing, when a peremptory knock came at the door, followed in a few seconds by its opening to reveal the Duke. He walked in, smiled at her and nodded dismissively at her maid, who, after a glance at her mistress, swiftly left the room.

"How dare you come in here like that and dismiss my maid!" exclaimed Imogen. "I'm not dressed to receive visitors! What can you mean by it?"

She drew her wrapper protectively across her bosom, thus accentuating its curves. Since it was green silk the exact color of her eyes, and her curls were in a disordered profusion on her shoulders, the whole gesture had the effect of making her look younger and even more desirable.

Ivo was much struck by her appearance, but controlled his impulse to take her in his arms and instead answered her question. "I mean to speak privately with you and did not think the presence of your maid expedient." He came more fully into the room and pulled up a chair. "By the way, here is your parasol. You left it in the boat when you ran away."

"I did not run away. I... I was overheated. I had been in the sun too long, and I should not have drunk that champagne. It made me dizzy."

"I agree you were overheated, but I am quite sure it had nothing to do with the sun. And the champagne may have added to it, but I think you were dizzy for quite another reason."

"And what, pray, might that have been?" asked Imogen, unwisely.

"Me," said his Grace shortly. "You wanted me just as much as I wanted you."

Imogen was stunned. She opened her mouth to speak, but no words came out. She sat motionless, staring at her visitor.

"Quite so," agreed the Duke, taking her silence as agreement. "And it is that I have come to talk about. Since we obviously have a strong mutual attraction, I propose that we spend the night together. If we both find the experience... agreeable, and I'm sure we will, I further propose that we throw in our lot together for our tour of Europe. We are both traveling alone and you are without protection. I can take care of that."

Imogen finally found speech. She stood up, her green eyes flashing furiously. "Spend the night with you? Travel with you? Have your protection? Good God, are you mad? The only person I need protection from is you! Whatever gave you the idea that I would welcome such an insult?" Her response was incoherent, as thoughts tumbled from her brain into her mouth. She said again, "Spend the night with you? I have never had a more...," she struggled for words, "a more... *revolting* proposal put to me! Go! Leave me at once!"

She looked magnificent as she gestured imperiously to the door. Ivo had risen, reflexively, when she stood up, and now stood, a look of disbelief on his face. Then he too spoke, his voice unnaturally calm.

"You are overwrought. Perhaps you were too long in the sun, after all. I know you cannot mean the things you say. I have never offered you anything but a sincere wish for your comfort and security, and I certainly meant no insult by my proposition. Quite the reverse. We will talk again tomorrow, when you are calmer. Good night, Imogen."

He left the room, closing the door quietly behind him. Then his anger became apparent. His lips set in a thin line and his eyes narrowed. He strode furiously towards the staircase, meaning to go down to the lounge for a brandy, or more than one. However, as he descended the stairs, he met the faded blond companion coming up. She fastened her eyes on his, with a look of enquiry. He raised his eyebrows and she nodded. He turned and she followed him back upstairs. When they arrived at his room, he opened the door and they both went inside.

After he left, Imogen had sunk back trembling into her chair, her hands gripping the wooden arms. Her heart was beating so fast she could hardly breathe. His words and her own whirled in her head. She had said the only person she needed protection from was him. He had said he meant only her comfort and security. She had said he revolted her. He had said he meant no insult. He had honestly appeared to think she would welcome his proposal. How could that be? Had she given him any indication that she would? She must have done. Then she remembered her mesmerized contemplation of him that afternoon. The dark hair of his chest, his strong forearms, the strength of his hands as he had lifted her into the boat. She remembered the almost irresistible urge to touch him, to fall into his arms, and her scrambled haste to get away from him. He was right. She *had* run away. Yes, she *had* given him reason to believe she would welcome his offer. What a fool she had been!

As the pounding of her heart subsided and she was able to think more clearly, she realized she would have to leave the hotel. The idea of facing him again made her shudder. She rang the bell for her maid, then sat at the bureau to write a note for M. Legrand. Her maid would take it to him. She informed him that she would be leaving first thing in the morning and needed to settle her account immediately. She would ask him to arrange a carriage back to Geneva as early as possible. She would have her maid pack her things tonight and they would leave before there was any chance of her having to face the Duke. She knew he fenced in the mornings and would in any case not expect to see her before luncheon.

This was all accomplished without any problem. M. Legrand was surprised and sorry to see her go and hoped that it was no lack of service at the hotel that caused her precipitate departure. She reassured him that it was quite the contrary. She had so enjoyed her stay that she had forgotten an important appointment with her man of business in London in two weeks' time. Her maid was startled at the sudden change in plans, but Imogen, giving her the same explanation, said with unusual asperity that she did not imagine she needed to explain her actions to her servant. She was, in any case, a simple Nottingham girl and was finding the whole Continental tour something of a trial. As a result, by eleven o'clock the next morning, Mrs. Mainwaring was well on the way to Geneva.

The Duke had no idea she was gone until she failed to present herself for lunch, and having again eaten a solitary meal, he went up to her room to find it empty, the bed stripped and the eiderdown, as was customary, hung out of the window to air. When asked, M. Legrand discreetly explained the reason Mrs. Mainwaring had given for her departure, and the Duke, too well bred to display any emotion, merely nodded and murmured that, of course, he had forgotten, but she had mentioned something of the sort. They both agreed that such a beautiful lady, an ornament to the society of the Hôtel Fleuri, would be sorely missed. She was indeed missed by everyone except the faded blond companion. This lady had met her as she was leaving the hotel and had given her a self-satisfied smile, accompanied by a slight lift of her brows, which Mrs. Mainwaring had interpreted, rightly, as a sign she thought herself to have succeeded where her competitor had failed. You can have him, Imogen had thought, and welcome.

After a day or two the Duke also took himself off, the company in the hotel, in spite of the willing ministrations of the faded blond, being decidedly flat. Over the next month he followed a circuitous tour through Italy into France, ending up in Nice, which was becoming a popular destination for the wealthy English escaping the gloom of the British weather. He arrived there towards the end of May, when the sunny days had settled in for good. In his light-colored suit, straw hat and Malacca cane, he became a common figure walking along where a shoreline promenade was being constructed. The local name for this was the Camin dei Anglès. Later, after Nice became definitively French, it would be called the Promenade des Anglais, since it was financed by the English church in Nice in order to give locals work after a particularly hard winter. The Duke would often stand in conversation with one or other of the workers, trying to dissect his speech, formed as it was by the constant intersection of the two neighboring cultures, as the ownership of the town swung between the Duchy of Savoy and the kings of France.

He found himself thinking quite often about Imogen Mainwaring and remembering with a rueful chuckle her comment in the Cathedral about the angler who talks about the biggest fish he never caught. He was not, of course, devoid of feminine company, some of it very delightful indeed, and enough to keep him in the south of France until the end of July. The King died at Windsor in June. A few weeks later, during three days in Paris, there was a revolution that overthrew King Charles X, the Bourbon heir, and saw the ascent of his cousin Louis Philippe. At that point, a sudden desire to be in England during the change in the monarchy, and a care for his own safety in those uncertain times in France made him, or rather, his valet, pack his bags and return to his estates in Buckinghamshire. There he stayed, reading about the changes at Court but prudently keeping away from London, riding over his estates, meeting with his agent and bailiff, visiting his tenants and generally behaving as an exemplary landlord. He still thought of Imogen, his emotion vacillating between humor and irritation as he remembered their brief time together, and especially the nature of their last encounter. He blamed himself, certainly, for having misread the signs, but blamed her too, for having been so mixed in her signals. A very odd woman, but, he admitted with a sigh, a fascinating one.

In October he received a letter from his lawyer in London. When he had settled in Nice, he had written to that gentleman informing him of his whereabouts and asking if there had been any resolution to the problem of the ill-fated duel. The response had been sent to Nice but, because of the momentous events happening in Paris, had been slow to arrive, had missed him, and had been re-directed. It had taken all these weeks to find him in Buckinghamshire. The letter informed him that the creepingly slow course of justice had ultimately completed its investigation and had exonerated the Duke of the death of his unfortunate opponent. Everyone, even that poor man's seconds, had declared that the whole thing had been an accident, caused in fact, by the other man's foolishness. His Grace was required to pay a fine for the infraction of having accepted a duel in the first place, which his lawyer had paid on his behalf, thinking to put the whole matter to rest as soon as possible. The Duke responded to this missive, explaining the delay and asking his lawyer to investigate the situation of the dead man's widow. He felt an obligation to help her if there were difficulties. In due course he received the answer that the lady in question came from a wealthy family and had already cast off her black gloves and shown herself in society, even at quite large parties or routs. It appeared the whole affair was all but forgotten. His Grace could return to London.

Chapter Six

Forced to spend the night in Geneva while she negotiated conveyance back towards England, Imogen remembered why she had not wanted to stay there in the first place. The company in the hotel was either puritanical-looking women with their husbands who appeared to think, even with her widow's weeds, or since they were so well tailored, perhaps because of them, that she represented a threat to their domestic happiness, or young men who leered at her, probably for the same reason. The first group pointedly gathered their skirts out of her path, presumably lest she contaminate them, and the second lay in wait for her at every turn and forced their undesirable attentions upon her. She therefore took the first means of travel out of the city she could find for herself and her maid and uncomfortably retraced her steps, at first by public conveyance. If she had had time, she would have written to her man of business and asked him to arrange the return trip, as he had done the outward one, but her rushed departure made that impossible. At one point, sandwiched between two burghers in a coach between Geneva and Lunéville and her maid forced to sit outside, she almost regretted not having thrown her lot in with the Duke, if only to enjoy his comfortable carriage. After that experience, she hired private carriages and proceeded in somewhat more comfort, though with no fewer difficulties.

Her chief problem lay in the fact that ostlers and postilions, not to mention innkeepers, were inclined to take advantage of a woman traveling alone with only her country-bred maid, where arrangements had not been made in advance. In some cases her beauty was enough to assure her fair treatment, but in many others it took all her considerable strength of character to argue, at first in schoolgirl French, and then in loud English, that she was not prepared to take the meanest room overlooking the stables, where she would be kept awake all night by carriages ringing on the cobbles and horses being changed. When ostlers sought to fob her off with broken-down nags to pull dilapidated carriages, she took to simply standing her ground and announcing "NO!" very loudly until something better was produced. When postilions demanded more money than had been agreed by the innkeepers, she found that, though she despised herself for resorting to such tactics, wailing tears and loud cries for help were usually enough to depress their pretentions. It took her nearly two weeks to arrive in Dover. By that time, she was exhausted and vowed never to set foot on the Continent again.

Her long journey had given her much time for thought. She spent many hours reflecting on the vagaries of her life that brought her to her present situation. She had been born an only child into a well-to-do upper middle-class family in Nottingham and had been raised with all the advantages of servants, governess, and dancing master. But her mother had died when she was sixteen and just beginning to think about her coming out. Her father had a sister married to a gentleman living in London, and this lady had invited Imogen to come and stay. She would be presented at Court, go to her debutante ball, and proceed along the conventional lines to procure a husband of her own rank, or preferably higher, and take her place in society. Her mother had done so, so had her aunt, and since, at sixteen, she was already a remarkably pretty girl, no one doubted her ability to do the same. But then her mother had died and her father had needed her to keep his house and look after him. He was several years older than her mother had been, and the death of his wife turned him overnight into an old man. At first, the idea had been that she would stay at home until she was seventeen, then eighteen, but after the third year, all plans for her coming out had been shelved indefinitely.

She had had numerous suitors, local men with greater or lesser fortunes, ready to spend them on so lovely a girl, but she had accepted none of them. She was not of a romantical disposition. She, like the other young women of her acquaintance, read the novels of Ann Radcliffe, particularly the *Mysteries of Udolpho*. But whereas they recounted with frissons of pleasurable terror the evil ways of Signor Montoni, who imprisons the heroine Emily in a tower when she will not marry the man of his choosing, she found herself asking why the heroine had not simply run away at once, before being imprisoned. When they swooned over the handsome Valancourt and rejoiced when at last Emily finds him, his wealth gone, living in a garret in Paris, she wondered what on earth they would live on. She felt that to be happily married, one needed, not a handsome but useless man lying in an attic with a torn shirt, but a spouse who was capable and *interesting*. None of the men who offered for her seemed remotely so. They were moderately good looking, moderately rich, their manners were patterns of moderation. How dull! So, one by one, they married the other young women in her circle, until she alone was left, living with her father and bidding fair to become a very pretty spinster.

Then, in her twenty-second year, her father died. She had known, of course, that she could inherit neither his home nor his fortune, but she had always thought that something would come along before that problem reared its head. Her portion was what her mother had left her, respectable pin money, but not enough to live on in the manner to which her upbringing had accustomed her. Her cousin Henry was the heir. He was the father of two young girls and husband to a wife whose chief pleasure was sitting on the sofa, chatting to her friends. Henry at once invited Imogen to live with them. The children would love to have such a pretty aunt to play with them. They might even be able to dispense with the services of a nanny. Imogen recoiled at the idea. She liked children well enough and would even have enjoyed having one or two of her own, but being nanny to someone else's, even her cousin's, held no appeal at all. Then her London aunt, who by now had lost her husband, asked her to come to live with her and be her companion. To be sure, her aunt's life was not very gay. She no longer went to many routs, and to no balls, but she was invited to her friends' homes for quiet afternoon card parties, not high stakes, of course. They went to occasional concerts at Willis's Rooms and had recently had a delightful evening of vocal offerings there. She was sure Imogen would be very happy living with her. Imogen's unhappy choices seemed to be: nanny to her cousin's children or companion to a dull, widowed aunt.

She was on the point of accepting the aunt, for London was, after all, London, when providence shone upon her. For many years her father had had a good friend in the town, a man some years younger than he, but still a good fifteen years older than Imogen. This gentleman, Fordyce Mainwaring, had seen Imogen grow up. He was a bachelor who had traveled a good deal and now went regularly to London. He seemed in tune with the fashionable life of the *ton*, even though he maintained his residence in Nottingham. He was out of town when Imogen's father died and when he returned, made haste to pay her a call of condolence. She was feeling very sorry for herself when he was shown into the parlor, and since she had known Mr. Mainwaring all her life, felt no qualms about telling him the cause. She made the melancholy remark that she would soon be moving from the only home she had ever known, to live a life with her aunt in London that promised to be dull in the extreme. It was either that, or stay and be an unpaid nanny.

Her visitor listened sympathetically and when she came to the end of her gloomy recital, thought for a few minutes before saying, "In that case, why don't you marry me? I promise to be neither dull nor infantile, but before you answer, there are some things I must tell you."

Imogen had spent many evenings with Mr. Mainwaring and her father, and she knew what he said was right: he was neither dull nor infantile. He could tell stories from his travels, knew gossip about London personalities and made them both laugh. She liked him very much. She did not think she loved him, but at least she found him interesting.

"The thing is, my dear, I am not interested in the... forgive me for being blunt... the physical side of marriage," said Mr. Mainwaring seriously. "If we marry, we will live as brother and sister. I will continue to conduct my affairs in London, and travel there quite often, but you will stay here in Nottingham. I will promise to care for you, to never tell anyone of our... arrangement, and to give you whatever I can. But you must accept what I am saying now. This will not change."

Imogen did not say a word. She got up and went to the window, staring blindly out into the garden. So now she had three choices, children's nanny, widow's companion, or a gentleman's almost wife. The silence persisted a full two minutes. Finally, she turned to her visitor.

"Mr. Mainwaring," she said, "I am very conscious of the honor you do me in asking me to become your wife, and I am glad to accept."

He bowed and replied, "Then you make me the happiest of men. I will send a note to your cousin today, asking to meet with him. You are of age and do not need his consent, but I feel it more proper to ask it anyway." He took her hand, kissed it, and was gone.

Imogen and Fordyce were married within the month and she moved into his home, not too far from where she had grown up. Her life changed rather little. She was mistress of a house for a man older than herself; she made sure his meals were as he liked them and that his every comfort was seen to. He, in return, cosseted her, admired her, and gave her lovely gifts of jewelry, for he had exquisite taste and consulted her on every matter pertaining to their life together. In one material way he added especially to her happiness. He insisted that she be dressed in only the most up-to-date of styles and materials. During his quite frequent trips to London he would buy the latest editions of the *Mode Illustrée* and swatches of cloth he thought suitable, and they would together choose gowns from the illustrations and decide on the best fabrics. His taste was impeccable. She learned from him what best became her and how to accentuate her lovely figure, eyes, and hair. He had a *modiste* in Nottingham measure her minutely and when he went to London, he would have the gowns made up to her exact size. She became the best dressed woman in town. Fordyce would chuckle to see other ladies try to copy her style, never with great success, as no one had her looks or his taste.

In spite of the limits of her marriage, Imogen was very happy. She was glad to be seen on her husband's arm at concerts, plays and social gatherings. His standing was improved by having such a beautiful young wife, and hers by having such an urbane and popular husband, for he was generous in his civic duties. He was a good-looking man of medium height and build, with a full head of steel gray hair, side whiskers and moustache. He was always beautifully dressed, like his wife, and despite the disparity in their ages, they were a handsome couple. Neither of them ever revisited the agreement they had made before they were married. Fordyce continued to visit London with regularity and Imogen stayed at home.

When they had been married about a year, on an impulse, Imogen asked whether she might go to London to see the sights and meet the *modiste* who had been making her lovely gowns.

"I would so like to meet her," she said. "I don't ask you to accompany me. I am not seeking to change our arrangement. It's just that I'd like to see her and thank her. She does such wonderful work for me."

"But of course you may go, my dear," responded Fordyce, "and of course I shall accompany you! I should have thought of it before. We shall stay at Mivart's in Mayfair. It's where I usually go, and they do one very well there. It's quite small, not the height of fashion, but elegant and comfortable. Let me write to them."

Accordingly, a month later, they set out to London in a coach and four. They changed horses and stayed overnight in

Cambridge. Imogen, who had hardly ever been outside Nottingham, found it all very exciting. Since the Inn was small and crowded, they occupied the same bedroom for the first time in their married lives, but they lay chastely side by side and enjoyed pillow conversation before they slept.

They arrived in London on the evening of the second day. The sky was fully dark as the coach rolled into town but the gas lamps gave it an extraordinary light. They had been introduced in the capital before Imogen was born and although at first there had been some nasty accidents with the new invention, most people now had them in their homes. Although they had gas lamps in Nottingham now, too, Imogen found it fascinating. London was so much more crowded. There seemed to be as many people abroad at night as during the day, and the fantastical shadows cast by carriages and people walking by looked like a vision from some sort of underworld.

The Mainwaring family had made its fortune in the handmade lace manufactories for which Nottingham was internationally known, but Fordyce had always been interested in industry and invention. As a young man he had invested some of his inheritance in the building of the Nottingham Canal which now linked the city with the Humber Estuary and thence the North Sea. He had done very well there and had continued to invest in new infrastructure when he had the chance. Although Imogen did not know it, because they rarely discussed business, he had also put money into the company that had brought coal gas to Nottingham some ten years before. His home had been one of the first to have gas lamps.

The Mainwarings were to spend a week in London, visiting the sights Imogen had heard of but never seen. They went first to the Tower of London, but naturally could not go inside as it was still being used as a prison. She learned that James I of Scotland had been held there before being transferred to Nottingham Castle, which surprised her, as she did not know Nottingham had a castle. She had lived there all her life without ever seeing one! Fordyce explained that there had been a castle on the promontory where the Duke of Newcastle had since built his great home. As she was not in the way of socializing with Dukes, she shrugged and forgot about it. She knew the story about the death of the little princes who were murdered in the Tower by their wicked uncle, another Duke, this time the hunchback Duke of Gloucester. He was later crowned King Richard III and was killed at Bosworth Field. "Served him right!" thought Imogen. She laughed at the story of the escape of the Earl of Nithsdale, whose wife and her maid visited him so often they confused the guards and he was able to escape dressed as a woman.

They went to St. Paul's Cathedral, the tallest building in London, through some of the dirtiest streets in the city. As they drove the carriage from Mayfair, it could be seen from way off, with its circle of colonnades and the stone lantern above, but they frequently had to hold their noses, especially when they drew near to the Thames, with its combination of sewage and floating rubbish from the hundreds of ships moored there. The magnificence of the Cathedral's interior made it worthwhile, however. It took Imogen's breath away, with Christopher Wren's rows of tall stone pilasters and Grinling Gibbons' wonderful wood and stone carvings. Fordyce, who was a fount of interesting information, told her that Gibbons was in the habit of carving a peapod amongst his profusion of flowers and foliage. He would leave the peapod closed until he had been paid, and only carve it open afterwards. They looked in vain for a closed peapod in the

Cathedral, but could fine none, so presumably he had been paid for his work!

Westminster Abbey was one of their last outings. The first thing Fordyce told her was that it was, in fact, neither abbey nor normal church, but a Royal Peculiar, responsible directly to the Monarch and not to the Archbishop.

"How very peculiar!" said Imogen, and they both laughed.

But it was not so surprising, since the Abbey had been the site of the coronation of all the English Monarchs since 1066, and their burial place as well. They wandered around, sat in King Edward's chair, looked at the stone effigies and, inevitably, in such a place where death was all around, each pondered the passing of people they had loved. Imogen found it interesting but not joyful, or even uplifting, as St. Paul's had been.

On their last morning, Mr. Mainwaring took his wife to the fascinating establishment called the Pantheon Bazaar. This was in the commercial district of Oxford Street, a large covered area with a number of different and fascinating businesses inside. It had been built some fifty years earlier and the main rotunda, with a central dome fancifully imagined to resemble the Pantheon in Rome, was the largest room in England at the time. Originally it had been intended for the superior entertainment of concerts and the dramatic arts, but over the years it had fallen lower in the social scale. Humorous plays, masquerades and costume balls had replaced the music of Mr. Handel and Italian opera, until the regulation of theatres imposed by the Lord Chamberlain had caused it to close. It was then reopened as a Bazaar selling everything from ribbons to rabbits. Imogen was entranced. She purchased a number of small items that would make excellent gifts for her cousin's wife and children, as well as for her maid and the housekeeper. That would be one less thing to worry about at Christmas time, she thought. Her husband, with his unerring taste, bought her a pretty bracelet of blue and green colored glass that would exactly match the new day dress they had ordered from the *modiste*. The gown would be of shot silk, which used bobbins of both colors to produce an iridescent fabric.

"Just a piece of trumpery, my dear" he said, "but I thought with your new gown...."

"How clever you are!" cried Imogen, kissing him on the cheek. "It will be perfect!"

The dressmaker Imogen so wanted to meet had been unable to see them until the last day. That afternoon Fordyce said he would leave her there to try on her new gown and look at illustrations and materials for future purchases.

"Take your time," he said. "I know how you ladies like to gossip. I'm sure there are all sorts of stories about society that you will hear. I'll return to the hotel by hackney and leave you the carriage. No rush!"

In the event, Imogen's comfortable cose with the *modiste* was interrupted in under an hour by Lady Jersey's arriving at the establishment and demanding to see the dressmaker at once. This lady was a good, if difficult, customer, and the *modiste*, begging Imogen's pardon, wondered if she could attend to her. Imogen at once agreed. Though she had never met her, Lady Jersey's name was familiar to her as being one of the most notorious women in London. Fordyce had once told her that Lady Jersey's many lovers had caused her husband to remark that if he were to fight a duel to protect his wife's honor, he would have to fight every man in London. She was known, however, to be generous and kind, especially to pretty young women new on the London scene. Imogen told the *modiste* that rather than keep the horses waiting any longer, she would take her leave. They had enjoyed a most useful and entertaining discussion. She would take with her the illustrations and fabric pieces proposed for her new gowns. Fordyce, whose opinion she valued more than any, would have the final say.

As she was leaving, a very good-looking dark-haired woman with a chestnut velvet hat from which a long and lustrous feather mane cascaded over one shoulder, came towards her. This must be Lady Jersey. Imogen curtseyed and smiled.

"Why, who are you? I don't know you, do I?" said the Lady. "I would have remembered someone as pretty as you. Are you new to London?"

"I am Mrs. Fordyce Mainwaring, my lady," replied Imogen. "I'm only here for a visit, in fact, we are leaving tomorrow, but I'm very pleased to have met you. I've heard so much about you."

"I'm sure you have!" smiled the other woman. "Fordyce Mainwaring? But I thought...," she did not finish the sentence.

"We have been married just a year," explained Imogen. "He was a bachelor for a long time."

"Of course, I see," said the Lady. "Well, when next you are in town, I'll give you vouchers for Almack's." With that, she bowed slightly and swept ahead.

Imogen could not wait to get back to the hotel and tell Fordyce who she had met. She wondered whether he would bring her back to London so she could go to Almack's. Perhaps she would ask him. She ran up the stairs to her room and dropped her packages. Then she went to the door that communicated with her husband's room and, after the briefest of knocks, burst in. She stopped abruptly. On the bed there were two figures, her husband and another younger man she did not know. She could only see the top half of her husband as he bent over his companion, but as far as she could tell they were both naked. His shocked countenance turned towards her over his shoulder and his face drained of all its color. No one said a word. Imogen turned deliberately around and went back the way she had come, closing the door quietly behind her.

She sat in silence in her room, forgetting her new gown and the designs and materials she had brought with her. She had led a sheltered existence and what she had seen was totally outside her experience. The only time she had heard of a man lying with another man was in the Bible, which she and her mother had read from cover to cover when she was a girl. She had not understood the reference and her mother had glossed over it, but she remembered the biblical condemnation. But Fordyce was a fine man, he had married her out of the goodness of his heart and had showered her with every kindness. Now she knew why their marriage was not a real union and why he traveled alone to London. She was shocked but she was not devastated. She could not condemn her husband. He had not deceived her; how could he have told her, an innocent girl, the whole truth? He had never pretended to be what he was not. Poor man! How unhappy he must have been all his life. She suddenly felt so sorry for him. She got up and went back to the communicating door. This time she knocked and gently called his name, then knocked again. After what seemed an interminable moment, the door slowly opened and Fordyce stood before her. He had put on some of his clothing, though he was in shirtsleeves and barefoot. In the background she could see the younger man, also now partially clothed.

"I'm sorry, Fordyce," she said, putting out her hand to him. "I'm sorry to have burst in on you. Please forgive me."

"Oh, my dear," he said earnestly, "how I wish this afternoon's work could be undone. I never meant for you to...."

"No! I'm glad I know the truth," she burst out. "You are my husband. You have always been so good to me. You must be who you are, and be happy, however you may achieve it. This changes nothing between us." She put her arms around him and kissed his cheek.

They stood like that for a long moment. Finally, he said, "You are very good. I could not have hoped for such understanding." Then, hesitatingly, "May I introduce you to Adrian, my... friend. He and I have been... together for some years now. He knows all about you. He would be so pleased to meet you."

Imogen moved forward and Adrian came towards her. He was a slim man with dark hair and very blue eyes. As he got closer, she could see he was older than she had at first judged. They took each other's hand and he bowed.

"It's sorry I am we had to meet in this unfortunate way," he said with a soft Irish burr, "but I am happy to know you at last. Fordyce has told me how lovely you are, but now I'm about seeing it for myself."

"And I am glad to know you, and to know that he has such a... a good friend. I'll leave you both now and go downstairs for tea. I won't bother you again." And turning to her husband, "Shall I see you for dinner? I've so much to tell you. I met Lady Jersey!"

Her husband accompanied her back into her room, "Thank you, my dear. I shall never forget your understanding and your kindness. Although I cannot be the sort of husband you deserve, I love and admire you." He kissed her hand. "Yes, let us meet here at half past eight and you can tell me all about Lady Jersey at dinner." He kissed her hand again and returned to his lover.

The next day they started home towards Nottingham. Imogen had very mixed feelings about her trip. Though it had been the occasion of the greatest shock of her life, it had been a wonderful trip. She felt she was a stronger person for knowing what she now knew, and in a strange way, she thought her marriage was on a more solid foundation.

Over the next months, she and Fordyce never discussed what had happened in London, and he continued to visit the city with regularity. His affectionate behavior towards her, if anything, increased, and he was constantly showering her with gifts. If at times she felt she was missing an essential part of what it meant to be a woman, she was able to tell herself that her life was far better than it would have been if she had chosen either of the other two options open to her after her father's death. She was never tempted to seek masculine company other than her husband's, both because of her own strict sense of moral obligation and frankly, because none of the men of her acquaintance interested her in the slightest.

Chapter Seven

Imogen and Fordyce continued this way for another happy year or so, until one late Autumn. Then, after Fordyce had been away in London for a few days and she was imminently expecting his return, she received instead an urgent letter from Mivart's Hotel to say that her husband had suffered an apoplexy and was hovering between life and death. She left Nottingham immediately and would have traveled through the night if she had been able, but when she sought to change horses in Cambridge and continue to London the same day, the landlord refused to give her the horses she required, saying the danger from footpads and highwaymen was too great, especially for a lady traveling alone with only her maid for protection. She spent an appalling night at the inn and continued as soon as it was light, but arrived in London to the sad news that her husband had passed away that morning. When she enquired if he had been attended at the moment of his death, since her greatest fear was that he might have died alone, she was told that his friend had been with him, the same friend who had been with him at the moment of his apoplexy and had only that morning left his side. They knew him only as Mr. Adrian. Imogen was glad that his lover had been with him, and would have liked to speak to him, but no one had any idea of his direction.

But worse was to come. It soon became clear that the staff of the hotel had formed their own opinion of the relationship between the two men, as one of the maids had come into the bedchamber where Fordyce lay, to find Adrian lying next to him on the bed, crying bitterly, kissing his hand and calling him "my dear." Rumor spread, as it inevitably will, until there was no one at the hotel, and Imogen feared, in the whole of London, who did not know it. Though her own maid would, she thought, keep her mistress's secrets, the hotel maids spoke to the stable boys, and the stable boys spoke to Imogen's driver and postilion, she could tell from their sideways glances and muttered comments that, quite soon, no one in Nottingham would be ignorant of it either.

Imogen sadly made arrangements for the transportation of her husband's body back home, and then for interment in his family plot. She placed a notice of her husband's death in the newspaper and, according to custom, had the servants cover all the mirrors in the house. Her husband's body lay in the front parlor surrounded by lilies, and she shared a constant vigil over the body with her housekeeper. During the day a large number of visitors filed past. He had been a popular and generous citizen of Nottingham, so his widow received all the dignitaries of the city. She could not help but notice the groups of men and women who gathered outside the house, talking in low voices, shaking their heads and shrugging their shoulders. She knew the rumors surrounding his death had spread and raged inwardly, but could do nothing.

She ordered a complete mourning wardrobe from her London *modiste*, modelled on the other gowns she had bought, but since this could not be ready in time for the funeral, she had one of her gowns dyed and purchased an appropriate bonnet. On the appointed day, the coffin was closed and taken from the house by carriage to St. Mary's Church in the heart of the lace making district, where the Mainwaring family had been so influential. The horses' hooves and bridle chains were covered with felt pads and they bore black plumes above their harnesses. Imogen walked behind the carriage, followed by other family members. A huge crowd came behind. The traditional service was followed by burial in the family plot and then Imogen was forced by custom to offer refreshments at their home. She was absolutely worn out by the time it was all over, both by the sorrow of losing a beloved partner and by the necessity of keeping a calm countenance in face of the whispered remarks and sidelong glances she saw on every side. Young as she was, she felt she had endured a lifetime of experience.

It took her some time to recover from it all, and she was still not receiving visitors when she received an unexpected letter. It read:

> *My dear Mrs. Mainwaring,*
>
> *You will know by now that I was with dear Fordyce when he suffered his first attack, and I stayed by his side until after his death. You also probably know that my intense and intimate sorrow was observed by one of the maids, who, I believe lost no time in spreading the story throughout the hotel, and probably further abroad. I am truly sorry to have created this most difficult circumstance for you and can only say in mitigation that my love for Fordyce as he lay at death's door was such as robbed me of any discretion.*
>
> *In the brief moments when he was lucid enough to speak, Fordyce spoke of you, dear Mrs.*

Mainwaring. He knew he would probably not see you again and asked me to convey to you his deepest love and admiration. He said you had brought a joy into his life he had not believed possible.

He also asked me to tell you that Martin Carter, his man of business in London, is to be relied upon to give you all guidance you will need in financial matters. As you are probably aware, dear Fordyce was financially very astute and involved in a number of ventures.

It only remains for me to express my heartfelt thanks for your understanding of the feelings that existed between your husband and myself, and to assure you, if assurance were needed, of my devotion to him, and to you.

With my deepest condolences, I am your obedient servant,

Adrian Brody

Imogen had heard her husband talk of Mr. Carter, and knew she would have to meet with him soon. Accordingly, she wrote to him asking him to wait on her as soon as he could conveniently travel North from London. He responded that he would do himself the honor of visiting her a week on Monday and stay in Nottingham for a few days, at which time he would not only share the contents of her husband's Will but also be able to present documents relating to his many business ventures. He duly arrived, a thin, fussy, somewhat stooped man with thinning fair hair. He was probably younger than he looked. His pale blue eyes were; however, extremely piercing, and before long Imogen began to see why Fordyce had placed such trust in him. With admirable clarity he explained both the terms of the Will, which, since Imogen was chief legatee, was quite simple, and also the varied nature of Fordyce's investments. Her inheritance was made up of a large fortune invested mostly in government bonds, which provided a steady though unexciting return. In addition, Fordyce had acquired shares in a number of new companies. These included, besides the Nottingham Canal and the Nottingham Gas Light and Coke Company, the Stockton and Darlington Railway, which in 1825 had been the first steam railway to carry passengers. Until then, railcars had mostly been horse-drawn and used to carry coal. The family fortune which her husband had inherited, said Mr. Carter, had been respectable, but he had multiplied it many times by judicious investment in developing industries. In short, Imogen was a very wealthy widow. There was an extra clause in the Will, however. Besides a few minor bequests, the sum of ten thousand pounds was left to one Adrian Brody, direction provided. She sought no explanation for this and none was offered, by which she understood that Fordyce's man of business knew more than he was saying.

They met every day for several hours, with Mr. Carter carefully explaining which funds were tied up and for how long, which funds were available to be moved, should more attractive placements be found, and which should be used for ongoing living expenses. Imogen had never dealt with any of this before. If she had needed money, Fordyce had simply given it to her. When she had bills, he paid them. It had been the same in her father's home. Now she was faced with the charge of managing the finances of the household. She learned how much coal was consumed, how the gas was paid for, how much was spent on household linen and laundry, the expense of employing the dozen persons who made up the staff, from the housekeeper to the boot black and the stable boy, the dizzying cost of keeping the stables and the horses. The outlay on food and wine seemed almost incidental.

However, Imogen discovered in herself a well of resourcefulness. After Mr. Carter's daily visits, she studied the columns and made a note of questions for the next time. By the time he went back to London, she felt comfortable enough to make a few changes here and there. With her husband gone, she no longer needed the services of his valet. Since this gentleman had been forty years with Fordyce, and was the recipient of one of the bequests, they agreed that his retirement was opportune. The fires in her husband's study and bedchamber need only be lit twice a week, to keep the places aired. The regular supply of wine from the merchant was also dispensed with. She herself drank very little and had no intention of giving dinner parties for many months. She could dispense with one of the carriages and corresponding horses. It was not long before she felt herself mistress of it all. Once she had the domestic finances under control, she thought she might look more closely at her husband's business interests. However, for the time being, she trusted Mr. Carter to keep the investments on an even keel, though he promised to apprise her of possible new ventures.

By the end of the month, her mourning wardrobe had arrived. She had ordered clothing in the same designs as had previously been made for her, but all in unrelieved black: four day dresses, three evening gowns, a walking dress and a traveling suit and a pelisse. She had already obtained from local establishments several lace caps, day and evening gloves, a lace shawl, and a warm wool shawl. She had had her milliner in Nottingham dye her bonnets and replace the ribbons with black. She had written a note to the jeweler she knew Fordyce had often used, asking him to wait on her at home. With him she talked over appropriate mourning items. According to custom, she had kept several locks of her husband's hair which had been finely braided. The jeweler recommended a brooch made with some of the braid, and a locket for the rest. On impulse, Imogen asked him to furnish also a gold necktie pin with a cabochon containing a small portion of the hair. This she sent with her condolences and best wishes to Adrian Brody, who received it with tearful gratitude and wore it every day of his life.

She had kept close to home in the meantime, both because of not having appropriate clothing and because of a desire to stay out of the limelight. However, she knew that it would appear odd if she did not both receive a few afternoon visitors and show her face at one or two small gatherings in Nottingham quite soon. She had received a number of black-edged notes from friends, desiring her to let them know when she was ready for visitors. Not being able to face a series of individual guests, and the inevitable searching questions, she decided to acknowledge them all at once with a quiet tea party. She would accept a couple of small dinner invitations. That was all.

It was enough. The tea party began in the accustomed fashion. She received her friends wearing one of her new gowns, a black lace cap and gloves. She was one of the rare dark-haired women who look very well in black. It rendered her eyes all the more startlingly green and her skin all the more like porcelain. It was therefore an exceedingly young and beautiful widow who received her guests sitting in an armchair, taking their hands as they arrived. It felt odd, but was normal behavior for the recently bereaved. The maids circulated with the tea and small sweets, and each of her friends joined her for a few minutes, as was the custom, circulating around until everyone had had the opportunity to talk privately with her. She was about half-way through this ritual when she began to notice groups of those who had already spoken to her sitting with their heads close together and occasionally raising their collective gaze to regard her both pityingly and appraisingly. It was clear that some piece of news had reached their ears. She did not have to guess what it was. She could not wait for the afternoon to be over; she had to steel herself to adopt as neutral a demeanor as possible as friends came and went, studying her closely for signs of distress, which they would, of course, have met with overweening sympathy. But she would not give them the satisfaction. At last, the final guest left. She had lingered in hopes of Imogen's unburdening her heart, but Mrs. Fordyce Mainwaring simply gave her a brief smile and thanked her for coming.

The first dinner party was worse. As she entered the salon, a hush fell upon those already collected, followed by a frenzy of chatter as people both sought to tell each other what they thought they knew, and beseech each other not to tell anyone else. At dinner, she was seated between a wealthy merchant who breathed whisky fumes over her, pressed her knee and muttered that if she was looking for a real man, he would be happy to oblige, and a clergyman, who likewise breathed over her, but with sanctimonious exhalations, and said in a low voice that if she needed counsel, he was available. When the ladies left the men to their port and repaired into the drawing room, there was a general sense of malaise, as if no one knew quite what to say, until Imogen herself brightly began a conversation about the price of coal. Since few of the ladies present knew anything more than that coal was used in fires, and had never seen a bill for it in their lives, this was doomed to failure. The men duly arrived and

Imogen hastily sat herself between two matrons, to avoid a repeat of her dinner conversations. One of the younger ladies entertained them with songs at the pianoforte, after which, Imogen pleaded a headache and took herself off. As soon as she was home, she wrote a note excusing herself from the second dinner party. She had mistaken the dates, she said. She was going abroad.

Chapter Eight

Ivo Rutherford, Duke of Sarisbury, strode into his club the evening of his return to London, to be met with cries of welcome or dismay, depending on the nature of the individual's relationship with him. His friends, who enjoyed his easy ways and sense of humor, were glad to see him back; those who were jealous of his unfair advantage of fortune, good looks and expertise with cards and women were disappointed, since their own success in the latter two arenas would be correspondingly less.

"Heard you'd gone abroad, Sarisbury," said one of his cronies. "How was it?"

"Fine, except for the French being at it again, replacing one king with another. Don't see the point. Though matter of fact I met old Louis Philippe a couple of times in Switzerland few years ago. He must be nearly sixty by now, poor old duffer. I understand he spent time as a waiter and can carve ham thin enough to read the newspaper through it. Useful attribute for a king!"

Everyone laughed.

"They exonerated you of blame in the duel, I hear," said another.

"Duel?" his Grace appeared to think for a minute. "Oh that! Forgotten about it. Yes, not my fault. Poor chap, that's what you get for trying to defend a lady's honor. Waste of time, if you ask me. If it needs defending it's usually because she ain't got any. 'Course, not being a marrying man, I don't understand these things."

To a chorus of shaken heads and chuckles, the Duke walked airily into the card room, where he stayed until the early hours, winning and losing a great deal of money with complete insouciance.

Over the next few weeks, he renewed his acquaintance with a number of fair Cythereans, or rather, they renewed their acquaintance with him, since he only had to appear at a gathering for them to find their way to his side. Esme, the wife of the slain husband, came to him with downcast eyes and a pitiful look on her face. She held out her hands.

"Your Grace," she said, "you find me a woman bereft."

Ivo bowed. "Didn't think you were that fond of him, to tell you the truth," he responded, matter-of-factly.

"But now he's gone I find myself so... alone." She lifted her tragic face to his. "I sit for hours, wondering how things... might have been."

"They might have been a damned sight easier for me if he hadn't been such a fool."

"I know, I know," cried the lady. "But I fear his love for me was so great, he abandoned all caution." Obviously, Esme knew her husband had acted imprudently and was interpreting it to her own advantage.

"Possibly," mused the Duke, "or it may have been he was so afraid of me that he lost his head. One will never know."

"Yes," said the lady, looking up at him, her piteous expression now replaced with something closer to coquetry, "it is easy to be afraid of you. You are so... big, and... strong. I remember." She allowed something like a shiver to course through her frame.

His Grace regarded her steadily until she had the grace to blush and drop her eyes. "Oh, come on, Esme," he said finally, a little more kindly, "get to the point. What do you want?"

"Want?" she said, her voice tremulous, "me? What could I possibly want... from you?"

"That's what I'm waiting for you to tell me."

"Why, nothing, I'm sure," she looked up at him again as she spoke. "I had only hoped that you might... like me again."

"I do... like you." The Duke was not encouraging. He had no intention of starting up again with this woman, "If you need financial help, I will give it to you. I will have my man of business contact yours. But that is all. You know as well as I do that our... friendship was over before the damned duel. Don't play the grieving widow with me, Esme, it won't wash. Find yourself another gallant. Shouldn't be hard. You're quite pretty,"

"Quite pretty?" Esme gulped. "You used to find me beautiful!"

"No, I didn't." His answer was repressive. "You were and are quite pretty and you were very eager. For both our sakes, don't play a Cheltenham tragedy! Looking miserable ruins your looks, anyway, so hold your head up, smile and you'll find it easy enough to get over it!"

Thus the Duke dealt with yet another of his lovers foolish enough to think he might really care for her. She went away then, furiously listing in her head all the names she wished she'd called him. But, as he had once told Imogen, he'd heard them all before, so even if she had said them to his face, he would have heard her with perfect equanimity.

Over the next few weeks even those most familiar with the Duke of Sarisbury's pursuit of beautiful women would have said that he was going beyond anything he had hitherto attempted. He seemed to appear every week with a different lovely on his arm and his reputation as a rake soared or plummeted, depending on your point of view. Some said it was delayed shock at having killed a man in cold blood, even if accidentally. Some said his enforced exile had made him hungry for the type of beauty only to be found in England. Whatever the reason, there were more women dabbing their eyes in corners or muttering imprecations against his name than ever before. He sailed through it all, as good humoredly charming as ever, with no shortage of others willing to try their luck in taming him.

It was in pursuit of just such another fair quarry that he found himself one Wednesday evening at Almack's. He very rarely went there, finding the low stakes gaming insipid, but Wednesday was the only day they had a Ball, and most Society women were there. The Patronesses held absolute sway as to who could be admitted by the issue of ten guinea annual vouchers only to those they considered worthy. Worthiness was not merely a matter of riches and rank. Nouveau riche merchants knew better than even to apply, and even those with a noble title could be excluded if their behavior was deemed déclassé. The Duke himself might have been amongst their number, had he not been so charmingly attractive and a personal friend of Lady Jersey. Their choices were capricious and inflexible, as were their decisions about what gentlemen should wear. The Duke of Wellington himself had been refused admission on one famous occasion, for not being properly attired. His Grace was therefore clad in the required knee britches, very much out of date, white cravat, and chapeau bras, which he found a damned nuisance. First of all, when worn, it made one look like a retired military man, and putting it down was impossible. It could not be put on a chair, since these were needed for the limited seating, and the foyer shelves were too small. One could hardly stand around all evening with it under one's arm, and it had to be dispensed with when dancing. In the end, the Duke put his under a chair, hardly caring whether it was kicked to bits or became covered in dust, highly likely as the Almack's rooms did not enjoy good housekeeping. The Patronesses were also adamant that the doors be closed at 11 o'clock, with no one admitted after that hour, and since the supper was only thinly sliced stale bread and butter and a plain cake, also far from freshly made, one had better fortify oneself with a good dinner before coming.

The Duke looked around from his superior height to find his latest quarry, a vivacious redhead. She had been married just over a year and was already tired of her husband, not surprisingly, as that individual was a pompous self-satisfied fellow with nothing to recommend him but a substantial fortune. As his eyes took in the assembled company, he beheld a figure he thought he recognized, clad in subdued lavender, and wearing the black cap and gloves indicating her widowed status. When she raised her head, his suspicions were confirmed. It was Imogen. The sudden flare of pleasure he experienced surprised him, as he had believed himself well over the disappointment of her rejection. He made his way towards her by degrees, stopping for a few words with friends here and there, unsure, and this also surprised him, of how to proceed. In the end, the decision was made for him. Imogen was seated between a slim man with dark hair, taken by the Duke at first for quite young, but who he could see, as he drew closer, was probably in his forties. On her other side was a stout elderly matron clad in black bombazine. They were engaged in conversation and none of them noticed him. Then Imogen looked up and saw him. Her eyes widened, but her expression remained blank. Then she deliberately lowered her eyes and turned her head away from him, back to her companions.

"So that's how it's to be," thought his Grace, with a feeling he recognized as anger mixed with disappointment. She was going to pretend not to know him. Well, two could play that game. He walked deliberately in front of her and her companions but afforded them not a single glance.

"What a very commanding figure of a man," whispered her aunt to Imogen. "How tall he is!"

"Yes, it must be very inconvenient," responded Imogen, smiling in spite of herself as she recalled the Duke's description of the discomfort of too-low furniture.

"That's the Duke of Sarisbury," said Adrian Brody, who usually accompanied them to these gatherings. "He is not someone you should be knowing, Mrs. Mainwaring. He has a dreadful reputation. One may see a different woman on his arm practically every day. Luckily, I doubt either your aunt or I have any mutual acquaintance with him, so we may avoid an introduction."

"How fortunate," murmured Imogen, though when she saw him, her heart had beat faster than she liked to admit.

The Duke soon espied the willowy redhead he had come to meet. She saw him at about the same time and made a languid path to his side. She had observed how other women had practically run up to him. They had not fared well. They had been seen on his arm two or three times, and then his attention had been turned elsewhere. She decided that an apparent lack of interest would serve her better.

"My dear Sarisbury," she said, as he bowed over her hand. "How insipid this gathering is! I do not know *where* one may go for amusement. Lord Pendleton has asked us down for a shooting party this weekend, but really, one sees all the same people, and I wonder, what is the point?"

"I imagine Dicky Pendleton's point is to get you into his bed before I do," said the Duke. "But we could steal a march on him tonight, if you like."

"How fearfully direct you are, Ivo—I may call you that, mayn't I?"

"Since it's my name, you could call me a lot worse."

"Ivo! You are funning me! You do not honestly think I would accept such a stark proposition? I'm not that easy, you know!"

"Funny, I somehow imagined you were! But it's up to you. Dicky Pendleton's a good enough chap. A little unexciting, perhaps."

She saw she had painted herself into a corner. If she refused him now, she might not get another chance. He was well-known for not asking twice. But she did not want to give in so easily.

"But my dance card is almost full! It would be too unkind if I were to disappoint those gentlemen!" She had been saving the last waltz for him anyway, as she knew how well he danced and what a fine pair they would make. "Will you not dance with me later and we can quietly leave before supper?"

"Quietly or not, it's all the same to me, but very well. Give me your card." He opened it and scrawled his name against the last waltz. Then he bowed again and left her to go into the gaming room, looking to where Imogen was laughing at something with her companions. He cursed under his breath.

Luck ran distinctly against him all evening. At length, hearing the dance-master calling for the last waltz he made his way, in no very good mood, to the side of the languid redhead. She had enjoyed a pleasant soirée, flattered by the many partners who had been delighted to dance with such a desirable partner. The Duke took her waist with scarcely controlled temper, which she mistook for passion. When he took her home afterwards, she was almost frightened, and then gratified by his powerful love-making, believing it to be a tribute to her own allure. She was wrong. His Grace was thinking of Imogen.

For her part, Imogen tried not to look at the Duke. She was nevertheless conscious all the time of where he was and saw him talking to the redhead. When they danced together, she could not forbear watching. They made a lovely couple, he so tall and she so slim that it made her appear taller against him. All at once, she felt disappointed in her undersized, and as she saw it, unattractively garbed self. She saw them leave together soon afterwards and guessed the conclusion of their evening. She had to pretend not to be disappointed.

Chapter Nine

After the welter of emotions she had experienced in Switzerland and her uncomfortable trip back from the Continent, Imogen had been only too glad for the peace and quiet in her own home back in Nottingham. She had picked up the thread of very few of her old acquaintances, remembering with a shudder the dreadful tea party and dinner that had provoked her departure. Her society comprised chiefly her cousin and his family and her best friend from schooldays, now married and the proud mother of a baby.

She spent many afternoons listening to her cousin's complaints about the problems of managing her unruly offspring as well as the household. Since she had a very competent nanny, and the little girls, when Imogen saw them, seemed to be models of placidity, and since she had retained the excellent housekeeper from the days of Imogen's father, Imogen found it hard to sympathize with her. When she asked her cousin whether she had tried the new smokeless coke for her fireplaces, which Imogen had decided to purchase because, although it was more expensive, it was much less dirty than coal, that lady looked at her in puzzlement and had no idea what she was talking about.

With her schooldays friend, conversation was more or less limited to a discussion of the wonders of Baby, who seemed to get colic more, teeth earlier and kick his legs stronger, than any other baby in history. Imogen agreed that he was a sweet little fellow, but had nothing more to say on the matter.

So it was not long before she began to be bored. She missed Fordyce's company, for he was always an interesting conversationalist. At the few dinner parties she went to, she always wished she could stay with the gentlemen and their port, when, she was sure, the real topics of the day were discussed, rather than leave with the ladies and sit through talk about how much tea the servants stole and how to get stains out of the carpet.

She had the idea one day of looking through the papers Mr. Carter had given her concerning her late husband's industrial holdings. Once she became accustomed to the dense prose of the documents, she became more and more interested in what she actually owned. She decided to subscribe to *The Times* newspaper from London, which arrived at least a day late in Nottingham but which provided her with the only financial information readily available. After a while, she found she could easily spend the whole morning poring over the news and articles. However, she was often frustrated when she realized that what she was reading about had happened days before. She began to feel out of touch in her provincial city and thought about how connections between London and the rest of England, well, Scotland and Wales too, come to that, could be improved.

She knew Fordyce had invested in the Stockton and Darlington Railway, and wondered what other railways there were. Then she read in *The Times* about the Canterbury and Whitstable Railway that had opened in Kent on the 3rd of May that year, in fact, just about the time she had been leaving Lausanne. The reporter had travelled on it. Imogen found his article absorbing and became fascinated by the idea of rail travel. Then she made up her mind. She would go to Kent and try it for herself.

She tried talking the idea over with her cousin, but he did his best to dissuade her. It was so far to Kent! It would be at least three days travel to get there, and probably more. She could not possibly go alone, and he was too busy to accompany her. The more he tried to talk her out of it, the more determined she became. Thinking it over, she decided her best course of action would be to make for London, stay there a day or two and then continue to Kent. She had stayed at her husband's hotel on her way back from Lausanne, but had felt very uncomfortable there. She wondered if her old aunt would receive her for a day or two. They had been in infrequent touch since her wedding, but their letters had been cordial. Aunt Dorothea had not blamed her one bit for choosing marriage over being a companion. Any girl would have done the same! The elderly lady had not felt up to the rigors of traveling to Nottingham for Fordyce's funeral, but had always said she would like to see her again. Accordingly, she wrote to her aunt, asking to be received for a few days at the end of the month. On impulse, she also sent a letter to Adrian Brody, saying she would be in London on these dates and asking him to wait on her, if he would be so kind.

As glad to be leaving Nottingham again as she had been to get back there three months before, Imogen made the trip to London in a much better frame of mind than on the last occasion, when she had been so anxious about her husband. The stop in Canterbury was quite pleasant. She had written in advance and was able to enjoy her dinner in a private parlor as well as to pass a good night in a quiet room. It was now midsummer and the days were much longer, so that when she arrived in London it was still quite light and the fantastical shadows that had amazed her before were almost invisible. Her aunt lived in a respectable but unfashionable part of town, in a house that had seen better days. It became clear that the elderly lady, with her almost as elderly companion, was at the point where she needed a great deal more help. Nevertheless, she was greeted with loving enthusiasm and made very welcome.

When she explained the purpose of her visit, however, her aunt cried out in dismay and shrank back in her chair in horror.

"But surely," she exclaimed, you cannot be going alone! It is unthinkable!"

"But aunt, my maid will be with me, and I traveled across Europe in just that way. I'm sure I can manage. At least they speak English in Kent! Besides," she was going to add, but did not, yet, "I hope I may have someone else to go with me."

The someone else was Mr. Brody. That gentleman had sent a note saying he would call on her, if convenient, the following morning. He duly arrived, dressed neatly but not flamboyantly in tan trousers with a dark blue jacket, not overly padded at the shoulders nor pinched at the waist, a waistcoat and white cravat, held by the pin Imogen had sent him. He thanked her again for it, saying it was his most valued possession. His blue eyes shone as he also told her that the legacy from Fordyce had enabled him to give up his job as a copyist in a lawyer's office, a job he had found soul-destroying. He could now concentrate on his painting. He was one of the many artists who had left Ireland because of the lack of patronage, and had sought to make a living in London. In fact, that was how he had met Fordyce. He had been lucky enough, on his first arrival in the city, to participate in a salon where he could expose his work. Fordyce had admired one of his canvases and had purchased it. Over the years, he had purchased others. They had become friends and… well, Imogen knew the rest.

"But those must be the landscapes we have at home in Nottingham!" cried Imogen. "Fordyce never told me they were yours. But, of course," she added, "we didn't speak of his… other life at all. I have always liked them. They are very, what's the word? Atmospheric."

"I don't know if you are familiar with Turner's landscapes?" asked Mr. Brody. "I've always admired them, and I've taken my inspiration from him. I hope my works are not too imitative. His are far finer than mine, of course, but, like him, I like to paint how a scene makes me feel, rather than a conventional view of it."

They talked in a serious fashion of the difficulties of supporting oneself as an artist, which was why Mr. Brody had taken the job in the lawyer's office. He knew, he said, that Fordyce would have given him money if he had asked for it, but he had never wanted to do so. He would even gladly have given him his paintings, but her husband always insisted on paying for them.

"Yes, he was a kind and generous man," agreed Imogen. "I hope he knew we both loved him very much."

They were both silent for a while, thinking of the man who had brought them together. At length, Imogen introduced the topic she had wished to see Mr. Brody about.

"I am very interested in the development of train travel in Britain," she said. "You may find it odd for a woman, but I have read as much as I can find about it, and now I wish to see it for myself."

She explained that she wanted to go to Canterbury and ride the train to Whitstable, then back again. Would Mr. Brody accompany her? She was prepared to go alone with her maid but knew from experience that a woman traveling alone often met with difficulties. There were bound to be wonderful land and seascapes on the way, which he might find inspiring. Mr. Brody was delighted to accept the proposal. He had never been into Kent. As she said, the views would no doubt be exceptional, and he, too, liked the idea of traveling on a train. So it was settled. Imogen introduced Mr. Brody to her aunt as an old friend of her husband's and explained that he would accompany her on her trip. Everyone was happy.

Fortunately, being both a very old city and the site of the famous Cathedral, there were guidebooks available for Canterbury. At a distance of sixty miles from London, the journey could be accomplished in a day if they began early. They would change horses at Maidstone. Some of the ancient city, said the guidebook, was still surrounded by a medieval wall, built over a Roman one. The West Gate Tower was worth a visit; it was the only one standing, the other gates having been demolished to make way for carriages. The medieval castle had, unfortunately, been destroyed over the centuries and only a shell remained. However, the Cathedral, famous for being the site of the murder of Thomas Becket, and the destination of the pilgrims in Chaucer's *Canterbury Tales*, was still intact except for the depredations it had endured during the dissolution of the monasteries.

Imogen read all this and remarked, "Isn't it interesting that there's all this history, and yet we are going to see the most modern of inventions! It just goes to prove you can't live in the past. I wonder if future guide books will mention the railway and it will be ancient history?"

Their journey went according to plan and they arrived in Canterbury in the evening. The guidebook had mentioned a couple of hostelries, and Imogen had written to secure rooms at one called *The Parrot*. The Inn turned out to be very old, built on Roman ruins in the fourteenth century. As Imogen followed the maid by candlelight up the creaking oak stairs into a room with a huge oak four poster bed that looked as if Queen Elizabeth could have slept there, she wondered again at the coexistence of the very old and the very new. She was so happy to be living in an age of invention!

On the morrow they made their way to the train departure point, which was in the north of the city. They climbed aboard a wooden carriage that looked not unlike a horse-drawn vehicle with iron wheels sitting on rails. There were holes in the floor, apparently for rainwater to drain. There was nowhere to sit; one had to simply stand and hold on. The engine looked like an enormous cylinder on its side, with a tall chimney stack at the front, from which issued puffs of steam and smoke, slowly at first, and then with more rapidity as the engine gathered speed.

The railway towards Whitstable ran uphill in three stages. Imogen was interested to see that the train's own engine could only pull the carriages easily along the flat. It had enormous difficulty pulling the train up the first gradient, and for the next two, stationary engines pulled the train up with ropes. At one point they went under a tunnel, and the smoke and steam from the engine blew back into their faces. Imogen was glad she was wearing black, as her gown would most certainly be that color anyway by the time they reached Whitstable. The whole journey took just over an hour; she was told afterwards it was about six miles.

They were not particularly interested in Whitstable, though it was a pretty enough fishing village. They ate luncheon at an inn close to the harbor and were offered oysters, for which the town was apparently famous, but they were wary of eating oysters in the summer and settled for mutton chops. As they waited to board the train for the return trip, Imogen talked to the engine driver. He was justly proud of his occupation, one of the few in the country, and of his *Invicta*, which was the name of his engine. She found it amusing that he referred to his engine as "she," but mused to herself that it was probably because he controlled her, as men have controlled women throughout history. When he told her of the occasional explosions that occurred because the steam was not properly bled off, she laughed to herself and thought that did indeed sound like a woman. She herself had been led to the point of explosion on more than one occasion, not least, she now thought with a pang, by Ivo Rutherford, Duke of Sarisbury. Try as she may to forget him, he had never been far from her thoughts.

On her return to London and her aunt's house, Imogen made an important decision. In order to keep her finger on the pulse of new industry and invention, she decided she had to be in London. She was no longer happy to receive the news one or two days late. Besides, Mr. Carter, with whom she would have to be in constant contact, was in the city. With his help, she would lease a house large enough to accommodate both herself and her aunt, and her companion. She would let her house in Nottingham, as she hated the idea of selling something that had belonged to her late husband. Her aunt, after initial misgivings about leaving a place she had called home for the past forty years, finally agreed, especially when Imogen told her that she would be looking only in the best parts of town, in Mayfair.

Fordyce had always told her, "Go for the best you can afford, my dear. Never settle for second best unless you have to, and even then, always be on the lookout to do better." She trusted his advice. She would have the best.

She met with Mr. Carter shortly after her return from Canterbury. He was astonished to hear of her trip there specifically to see the new train service. She explained her interest in the burgeoning railway industry and asked him to look for business opportunities in it.

"There are obviously problems that need to be addressed," she said. "At present, the steam engine is incapable of pulling even a quite short train up any sort of incline. The *Invicta*, which I believe to be the most recent self-propelled steam engine available and manufactured by a Mr. Robert Stevenson, will need to be made more powerful. And there are issues with steam pressure that need to be studied. Nevertheless, if it were possible to purchase shares in his company, I should like to do so. In addition, if there is a new railway planned somewhere, I would be interested in acquiring shares. Can you look into it? My own resource is *The Times*, which tends, of course, to report after the fact. But perhaps you have other contacts."

Mr. Carter blinked. He had never had any woman sit where Imogen now sat and ask him to look into any questions of business, least of all a young and beautiful woman like Mrs. Mainwaring. He knew, of course, that her husband had invested a few years before in the Stockton and Darlington Railway, the first steam driven railway, which, though it had carried passengers on an initial journey for advertising purposes, was mostly used to carry coal from collieries to the ports. That had been a lucrative placement. But she had obviously studied the question and knew more about it than he, so he simply cleared his throat and answered, "Of course, Madam."

"Then there is the question of renting a house for myself and my aunt and her companion. I am moving to London, where I can be closer to… to where things are happening. I will let the house in Nottingham. You may leave that to me. But since I don't know London at all, I will need your help in finding something suitable. Nothing too small or out of the way. I want to have a good address with large rooms. My aunt will want to hold card parties and the like. I do not anticipate entertaining myself, at least, not while I am in full mourning. But my dear husband would not have liked to see me in anything mean and shabby."

Again, Mr. Carter blinked. He knew she was right about her husband. He had been a man of taste and discernment, not least, it now appeared, in the choice of a wife. And yet he had been… Mr. Carter did not name to himself what Mr. Mainwaring had been. He had been a clever man, and a good one, that is all one needed to remember.

"It will be a pleasure to do what you ask. I will put out feelers in respect of new… placements in the railways, and see about procuring a suitable habitation for you. When do you return to Nottingham?"

"Tomorrow or the next day. I see no point in delay, since I have made up my mind." She gave her man of business a brilliant smile. "I feel I am on the brink of a great adventure, wish me luck!"

"I do, Mrs. Mainwaring," he answered sincerely, "indeed I do!"

In this happy frame of mind Imogen returned to Nottingham to settle her affairs there before beginning her new life in London. Needless to say, her cousin was not at all encouraging.

"But you have nearly no acquaintance in London, Imogen," he said, reasonably. "How will you go on? It is not easy for a woman alone, you know."

"It has not been easy here with the way people have treated me after poor Fordyce's death," she retorted. "I've been an object of gossip, or pity, or in the case of several gentlemen, of undisguised lechery. It can't be any worse in London. At least it's so large that no one will care about Fordyce, or what he was, or me and what I am."

He was shocked. "It's not becoming for you to talk in such a manner, cousin. I'm sure you have misunderstood the matter. No one wishes you anything but the best."

"The best person to talk about behind her back, you mean, or to shake their heads over. Anyway, it's no good trying to dissuade me. My mind is made up. My man of business is already working on it."

Her cousin shook *his* head and tried to get his wife to talk some sense into her, but since that lady's only feelings in the matter were that Imogen would no longer be available to entertain her girls, and represented to her how much she would miss them, her words fell on deaf ears.

"I'm not going away forever!" she cried at last. I will come back from time to time, and you may come to London to see me!"

That aspect of the matter had not occurred to her cousin-in-law, who now perceived the advantage of having a free place to stay in the Metropolis, and rapidly began to calculate how soon she could expect to make the trip.

"Of course," said Imogen hurriedly, "I don't yet know what type of house may be found for us, and how many bedrooms it may have, perhaps only three. But for a short stay I am sure something may be contrived, if you don't mind the girls sharing with you."

Since this prospect was far from pleasing to the loving Mama, the question was, for the moment, dropped.

Chapter Ten

Letting out her house in Nottingham proved surprisingly easy. Since Fordyce had applied to himself the same advice he had given to Imogen about always buying the best, he had built his large house in the best part of town, slightly above the city and enjoying a fine prospect over the countryside from one angle and the town from another. It was situated in its own grounds, with mature shady trees and flower beds that bloomed from spring to autumn.

A Mr. Hawksley from the Trent Waterworks Company presented himself as a prospective tenant, and Imogen was interested to learn from him that his company was in the process of working to supply constant pressurized water to the homes of the city. Running water was available in other cities but only by means of intermittent service from cisterns. Constant water had been considered unfeasible due to the deterioration of fittings and faucets. However, Mr. Hawksley had developed fittings he believed to be robust enough to withstand the water pressure, and was trying to persuade the plumbers of the city to use them. He expected the project to be completed within the next year. Imogen gladly let the house to him and then wrote to Mr. Carter instructing him to buy shares in the Trent Waterworks Company.

In London, meanwhile, Mr. Carter had found a house he thought might suit her. It was at the end of a terrace of houses just off Park Lane, in a fashionable but quiet, leafy area. It was not over-large, but it had good proportions and a fine outlook over the trees of the park. It was accessed by a set of wide stone steps up from the street which led to the first floor, where there was a wide foyer and three quite grand rooms: a drawing room, a dining room, and a library, together with a smaller family room. From the foyer, a curved staircase led upstairs to four large sleeping apartments. The kitchens and utility rooms were in the basement. This could be glimpsed down between the wrought iron railings on either side of the front steps. The servant's quarters were, as was customary, on the third floor, accessed by a back staircase. The mews behind the terrace housed the stables with ample room for her carriages and horses.

Imogen instructed him to take a lease for a year, with an option to extend, and set about packing up her Nottingham home. She had no qualms about taking everything from there down to London. On the one hand, everything her husband had bought for his home had been of the best, and on the other, Mr. Hawksley had three young children whom she did not care to envision climbing all over her Hepplewhite pieces. Fordyce had admired this classic style, but once told Imogen that in all likelihood none of it had actually been made by George Hepplewhite himself. In fact, his style had only become popular after his death in 1786, when his wife published *The Cabinet Maker and Upholsterers Guide.* There were even some people who thought she was George! They had both laughed over the idea, but Imogen thought it not unlikely that a woman would have designed the pieces. They were sturdy, practical and comfortable to sit on, pretty to look at, but not as hard to keep dusted as the designs of, say, Thomas Chippendale, ornamented with all those curlicues.

In any event, she had it all packed up, together with the Turkey rugs and Adrian Brody's mysterious landscapes, and moved the lot to Park Lane. She invited her aunt Dorothea to move in with her and bring whatever she wished for her own and her companion's apartments, and for the family room.

It took a few weeks for the ladies to settle in. Mr. Carter was very helpful in the matter of new servants, since all of Imogen's staff had stayed at the house in Nottingham, except her personal maid, who was glad to leave. The trip to the Continent, though she had found it uncomfortable at times, had broadened her horizons as well as her mistress's. Aunt Dorothea's servants had been, for the most part, nearly as old as she was herself and preferred to retire with Imogen's generous bonuses. Everyone was delighted with the new accommodations, and being close to the fashionable part of London.

Imogen told herself that with her new life, she could now dress in part-mourning. Her husband had been gone nine months, and it was time. She would never forget Fordyce, in fact she thought of him every day as she pored over *The Times* in the library, which became her *de facto* sanctuary. He had had their portraits painted when they were married, and they now hung there. She often silently asked him whether he thought this or that looked like an interesting placement, and when she saw the price of stock she had acquired moving up, she would say out loud, "Well, Fordyce my dear, what do you think of *that?*"

Now she was living in London, it was easy to visit her *modiste* and order another new wardrobe. She knew he would have approved of the beautiful silk and fine wool gowns she and the dressmaker chose. These were perfectly tailored to her shape, in shades of lavender, lilac and purple that enhanced the green of her eyes. She continued to wear the lace caps and gloves, but with bonnets matching her gowns, and the black lace and shining curls peeping out underneath the upturned brims, she looked more lovely than ever.

So there she was. In under a year, Imogen had gone from being a married woman, her every whim provided for by someone else, to an independent widow with a new home, in a new city, with new household, and, above all, an absorbing new interest. Even aunt Dorothea seemed filled with new vigor.

"Imogen, my dear," she said one day as they sat at the breakfast table, where Imogen was opening her letters, these days mostly prospectuses of new companies she had asked Mr. Carter to procure for her, "it's all very well for you to spend your days looking at all those documents, though what on earth they are talking about is beyond me, but it's not good enough!"

"What isn't good enough, Aunt?" asked Imogen, distractedly, her mind going over a prospectus she had just read for a company proposing to replace the macadam on London streets with wooden blocks.

"Sitting at your desk all day and not going out, meeting people," she did not say, "even a new husband," though that's what she thought. "You're too young and pretty to be looking at... whatever it is you're looking at!"

"I don't think it's a good idea, anyway. Wooden blocks will wear out even quicker than stone. And think how slippery!"

"For goodness sake, we are not talking about wooden blocks! We are talking about your going into Society, having a little amusement. Fordyce would not have expected you to remain in mourning forever!"

Imogen laughed and protested that she found wooden blocks amusing, but later that day, as she stood up to stretch her legs, from having been seated too long at her desk, she remembered her aunt's words. She supposed it was a little unnatural, hardly ever going out in the evenings. She filled her days easily enough with her business investigations, and occasionally visiting art galleries with Mr. Brody or going back to the Pantheon Bazaar, though that place, she reflected, seemed to have gone downhill. Apparently, masquerade balls were now held in the Pantheon itself, and they degenerated into sad romps. It came to her then that Lady Jersey had said she would give her vouchers for Almack's. An evening there now and again would be a diversion, and she thought her aunt, with her newfound energy, would enjoy it. But it had been over two years since she had met Lady Jersey at her *modiste*'s. Would she remember her? On an impulse, she sat and wrote a note.

> *Dear Lady Jersey (it ran),*
>
> *I hope you will forgive me for presuming upon what was a very fleeting acquaintance. We met at Madame Angela's a little over two years ago. At that time, you were kind enough to offer to give me vouchers for Almack's, should I find myself in London. I am now living in the Capital, my husband having passed away nearly a year ago. May I have the pleasure of waiting on you at your convenience?*
>
> *With grateful thanks, I am,*
> *Yours sincerely.*
> *Imogen Mainwaring (Mrs.)*

Almost by return of post she received a note from Lady Jersey, inviting her to tea on the following Wednesday.

Imogen arrived at the appointed hour at 38 Berkley Square, a bow-fronted residence in one of the best known of London's squares. When she was introduced into the salon, Lady Jersey rose to meet her with a charming smile and outstretched arms.

"My dear Mrs. Mainwaring! Of course, I remember you now! When I received your note, I had a memory of our encounter, but I had forgotten how lovely you are. Please do sit down."

Once they were seated and tea had been poured, her ladyship continued, "But I see you are not quite out of mourning. It's too sad to see someone so young wearing the weeds. It's been almost a year, you say? Then I should throw them off at once! You cannot hope to catch a man wearing even half-mourning, as becoming as it is on you. It's just too, too, off-putting for them. Probably makes them think of their own mortality!" She went off into a peal of laughter. "The poor dears are so concerned with the idea of a loss of, let us call it *vigor*, sometimes it's really quite comical!"

Imogen could not help joining in the laughter, though a gentleman's vigor, or lack of it, was something quite outside her experience. However, according to all reports, Lady Jersey was an expert.

"I have only just put off my black, so I shall continue as I am for a few more months." She replied at last. "I am not looking for a man. I have quite enough to do without looking after a husband."

"My dear! I wasn't talking of a *husband*! One of them is more than sufficient! But you will want someone to take you in on his arm, to bring you sherbert, call your carriage, that sort of thing and of course, should you want more…."

"Oh, I have a friend who will do that… or most of it," Imogen interrupted, blushing. "He's an old friend of my husband, a most talented and charming Irish artist."

"I see," said Lady Jersey, looking directly at her, so that Imogen thought she really did see, "Well, you must ask him to make an application for vouchers. If he is as charming as you say, there should be no difficulty, but the other Patronesses and myself are very careful about the gentlemen we invite."

Imogen promised that she would ask Mr. Brody to call on the ladies of Almack's, and soon left with vouchers for herself and her aunt and her aunt's companion. She insisted on paying the annual fee for all three. She could easily afford it.

Adrian Brody duly presented himself to Lady Jersey and was easily able to procure vouchers. In fact, the Patronesses had a soft spot for displaced Irish artists, who, while not uncommon in the city, brought with them a breath of different air as well as their delightful brogue. It was therefore no more than a couple of weeks later when Imogen, her aunt and Mr. Brody went for the first time to Almack's. Still wearing half-mourning, Imogen was clearly not there to dance, but the three of them very much enjoyed watching others disporting themselves. They were highly amused by the airs adopted by the young Pinks of Fashion, who seemed to delight in performing complicated steps, especially in the Gavotte.

They were laughing at one such exhibition when The Duke of Sarisbury saw them on his way to the card room. He was surprised that seeing her laugh, apparently oblivious to him, touched him on the quick. He would have been happier had he known that, in fact, she was very aware of his every move. She saw him talking to the lovely redhead, saw him go into the card room, saw him dance with her later and saw him when they left together. She told herself she did not care.

Chapter Eleven

Once Imogen had been seen at Almack's, and through the offices of Lady Jersey had been introduced to a number of society ladies, she began to receive more invitations to routs, parties, and balls than she could have dreamed possible. She was usually accompanied by Mr. Brody, who was soon recognized as her companion, not her lover. If the circumstances surrounding her husband's death had at any time caused a ripple on the London scene, it certainly had ceased by now to be of interest and she was simply recognized as a very young well-to-do widow.

By some mysterious osmosis of understanding, akin to that of families of monkeys in the African jungle, her comfortable financial status appeared to be well-known. As a result, she had to pour cold water on the pretentions of many an admirer, both of her own age and older, who were doubtless attracted by her beauty but still more interested in her fortune. It was a truth universally accepted that a lovely young woman of means must perforce need a husband to take care of both her and her money. Adrian Brody became very adept at recognizing these fortune hunters at fifty paces and more than once whisked her away from under the nose of a pretender by claiming a dance which was not listed on her dance card, or an engagement that dear Mrs. Mainwaring had unfortunately forgotten.

Their laughing friendship did not pass unremarked, especially by the Duke of Sarisbury, who, to his increasing frustration, Imogen steadfastly refused to acknowledge. He had gone so far as to ask Lady Jersey to introduce him to her formally, as if they had never met, but when this at last occurred, Imogen had simply given him a brief curtsey, muttered a polite word of acknowledgement and immediately left them both on the pretext of a pressing, though vague, engagement. He had been given no opportunity for conversation with her at all. No woman had ever treated him this way before, and he vacillated between a desire to ignore her in return and to force her to speak to him. He decided at length on the latter.

Almack's was made up of a large room in which people could either sit and watch or participate in the dancing, together with a dining room and smaller rooms behind for card players and billiards. Rather in the manner of a theatre, there was a balcony and a number of smaller boxes overlooking the main floor. These were accessed by a wide staircase festooned with rather dusty hangings that provided embrasures for anyone seeking privacy.

The Duke had noticed that Imogen had taken to installing her aunt in one of the upstairs boxes, no doubt to give her a better view of the activities below. He therefore waited in one of the embrasures until he saw her descending the stairs alone, whereupon he seized her around the shoulders, and, with his hand over her mouth, drew her none too gently into his arms within the privacy afforded by the curtains. She was too shocked to struggle until she saw who it was, when she began to writhe, her eyes firing sparks at him.

"I find your struggling against me quite delightful, so by all means continue," said the Duke in a low voice, "but if you promise not to scream, I will remove my hand from your mouth."

Imogen immediately stood still and nodded her agreement, though her eyes were still furious. Ivo took his hand away, but still held her tightly against him.

Angry with herself at the undeniable pleasure she felt at being held in the Duke's strong arms, she said in an angry whisper, "Let me go, you brute! What on earth do you think you're doing?"

"I'm forcing you to speak to me. So far, it seems to be working," responded the Duke, without, however, relaxing his grip.

"I have nothing to say to you. Let me go! How dare you?"

"I dare because I have wanted to speak to you ever since you ran away from me in Lausanne."

"I didn't run away from you," said Imogen unconvincingly. "I... er... I remembered an important appointment in England."

His Grace simply raised an ironic eyebrow and smiled. "As I say, I've wanted to talk to you since you ran away, and this seems to be the only option."

"Very well, then, say what it is you want to say, and let me go. My aunt will be wondering where I am." Imogen relaxed a little in his arms.

"I want to talk to you properly, not just have a few words behind a drapery. Will you meet me later this evening. Or tomorrow?" Ivo adjusted his grip into something closer to an embrace.

"No, I most certainly will not. I can't imagine we have anything to talk about in any case."

"How can you say so? Did we not have a delightful time in Lausanne? Did you not enjoy my company? I have the most pleasant memories of our time together and I cannot believe I'm alone in that!"

"I admit we did have a very pleasant time, and I enjoyed your company, until you offered me the incredible insult of what I believe is called a *carte blanche*. That has spoiled our friendship forever."

"You are refining too much upon it! I offered you what many other women would have leaped at. You know I am not a marrying man, and my offer was the best I have. I meant no insult by it, quite the contrary!"

"Then you are so sunken in debauchery that you do not know the difference between an honest woman and a false one."

"Sunken in debauchery?" his Grace let out a shout of laughter. "I admit I enjoy the company of women, but debauchery, never - well," he amended, "hardly ever. I don't believe you know the meaning of the word." He ignored her protests and continued. "Come, Imogen, we can deal better than this. Will you not acknowledge our friendship, dance with me, allow me to escort you here and there? I even promise not to repeat the proposal that was so distasteful to you."

"No, Your Grace," replied Imogen firmly. "No, I will not. Any woman seen with you will inevitably be tarred with the same brush as the others. I do not wish to be considered in that company."

"But this is ridiculous! I miss you, Imogen! Your company, your conversation, your laugh!

"You miss me!" Imogen laughed scornfully. "For how long did you miss me the last time I saw you?"

"Why, until now!"

"What did you do immediately after leaving me that night?"

"I went to bed."

"Alone?"

"Er…," his Grace hesitated.

"Am I not right in thinking you… entertained the blond companion of that old lady?"

"Well, I may have… she was very…."

"Precisely. And when you left Lausanne, did you spend some time alone reflecting on why I had refused you?"

"No, I thought you were overwrought and not yourself."

"Did you adopt a celibate lifestyle?"

"No, why should I?"

"Because you were missing me, or so you say. Just as you have been missing me since you got back to London. How many women have helped you to miss me? Let me see, in the last month alone I've seen you with a willowy redhead, a golden beauty, perhaps not altogether natural, a tall brown haired lovely, oh, and yes, that young woman who is so fair her hair is almost white. Those are the ones I've seen, and there are probably others. I can see you've missed me very much!" she ended sarcastically.

"I'm happy to see you've noticed my paramours!" replied his Grace, giving her a squeeze. "It gives me hope that you are not altogether unmoved by me."

"Stop squeezing me like that! You know you are impossible to ignore, as tall as you are, and besides, I believe you deliberately paraded them in front of me!"

Since this was precisely what Ivo had done, he did not answer this charge.

"Now let me go, Your Grace," said Imogen into the silence. "You can see that what you propose is impossible. I will not be added to the list of your paramours, as you call them. I will not have my name joined with theirs. It is the name of a man who was a true gentleman who cared for me very much."

The Duke smiled ironically. It was on the tip of his tongue to say, "A man who preferred other men." But he did not. Instead he said, "I will let you go after I've kissed you."

"No! What gives you the right to kiss me?" replied Imogen in an urgent whisper and struggling again against his grip.

"The fact that you have allowed yourself to stand in my embrace for the last ten minutes. That is usually signal enough for any man."

"I did not stand willingly in your embrace! You said you liked it when I struggled, so I stopped, that's all."

"There's a very nasty name for women who lead men on and then deny them their reward. I won't call you by it as, in spite of what you think of me, I am a gentleman. But I demand my kiss."

With the arm around her waist, he pulled her closer and put his lips to hers. Imogen remembered them from the kiss in the cathedral stairwell: somehow soft and firm at the same time, and, though she hated to admit it, wholly wonderful. Then he touched the tip of his tongue between her lips as he had done before. Her heart leaped into her throat and she felt her nipples harden. He must have felt them too, as he brought up his hand and ran it lightly over her left breast. She gasped and pushed him away.

"St… stop it, stop it, Ivo," she said, in her confusion using his Christian name. "Stop it, I don't like it!"

"Oh yes you do." He replied with a chuckle. "I think you like it very well indeed. You may pretend to be indifferent to me, but we both know the truth is otherwise. When are you going to accept my offer? It still stands."

"Never!" Imogen was furious. "I shall never accept your offer. I told you before, I consider it an insult. Just because you are stronger than I, it does not give you the right to take advantage of me. But I should have expected it of someone like you. You may have a title, but you are not a gentleman. My husband was twice the man you are."

The Duke stiffened. He dropped his arms and controlling his anger, said quietly, "In that case, I shall importune you no longer. Good night, Mrs. Mainwaring." And with a bow, he was gone.

The Duke rejoined the crowd downstairs, but did not stay there. He hesitated for a moment, but since the only beverages served were a very tart lemonade and a tea hardly worth the name, and his Grace desired strong drink, he strode out of the place. He went directly to his club, where he proceeded to get royally drunk. He was helped to his carriage by the club porters in the early hours, and his butler and valet managed to get him up to his bedchamber. His anger had by then left him and he was inclined to be maudlin.

"She doesn't want me. Thinks I'm no gentleman and I'm debauched," he muttered to his valet, who was attempting to remove his boots. "Am I debauched, Davis?"

"Not exactly debauched, Your Grace," replied his man, the only person alive who could tell him the truth when he did not want to hear it, "but not exactly a model of sober behavior, are we?"

"I should think not! Sounds like a dead bore! But you think that's what she wants?"

"I think it's what all ladies worthy of the name want, Your Grace."

"God dammit!" said the Duke, and fell asleep.

After leaving the Duke, Imogen had walked slowly back up the stairs, trying to collect herself. After walking back and forth in front of their box once or twice, she had regained her equilibrium and went in to rejoin her aunt, who was being very enjoyably entertained by Mr. Brody. Unlike his Grace, she reflected ironically to herself, they did not seem to have missed her. Together they were laughing at the antics of some of the young tulips on the dance floor. In the corner of the box, a youthful individual with a shock of fair curls falling over his forehead was writing furiously on a pad. He looked up as Imogen entered.

"Ah! There you are, dear Mrs. Mainwaring, or may I at last call you Imogen? I've been waiting this age to see you. I'm working on my Epic Poem." He spoke the last two words with obvious capital letters.

"Lord Fairclough," smiled Imogen, glad of this diversion. "I don't think Christian names are appropriate. I'm sure your Mama would not approve."

"Oh, Mama approves of nothing! She wants me to finish up Oxford, but what good is that to me? I live only to write poetry, and for that, you need *experiences*, not study!" He looked at her earnestly. "If only you would marry me, Imogen!"

Evidently the interdiction against using Christian names carried no weight with the young artist, any more than it had with the Duke.

"But you are not of age! And when you are, you will have forgotten about an old lady like me. Let us just be friends!"

"Friends!" he spat contemptuously. "I don't need *friends*, I need *experiences*. Let's just go to Gretna Green and be married. Once we are wed, Mama will just have to accept it. I'll be twenty-one next year. They have to let me have my inheritance a few months early if I have a wife to support!"

"Lord Fairclough, Desmond," said Imogen gently. "You must see I am still in mourning! Even if I wished to be married, which I do not," she added quickly as he started up, "it is impossible. Besides, you do not wish to marry someone of whom your Mama cannot approve. Be sensible!"

"Poets are never sensible!" retorted her lover. "If they were, they would never write anything! Poets must be mad! They must defy convention! Haven't you read the sublime words of Mr. Coleridge:

> *And all should cry, Beware! Beware!*
> *His flashing eyes, his floating hair!*
> *Weave a circle round him thrice,*
> *And close your eyes in holy dread*
> *For he on honey-dew hath fed,*
> *And drunk the milk of Paradise!*

"Yes, I see," said Imogen prosaically. "But do you really want to have flashing eyes and floating hair? You really are much nicer as you are. You have lovely blue eyes and your fair curls are adorable."

"Do you think so, Imogen?" said the poet in deadly earnest. "If you like them, I shall never cut them again. Though Mama won't like it! She says I shouldn't let my curls fall in my eyes."

"Well, your Mama isn't a pretty girl who will be enchanted by your curls. Look, there's one there." She gestured over the balcony rail. "The poor thing is sitting all alone. Do go and ask her to dance. Please, just for my sake!"

"That's Anne Robertson! I knew her when she was in short skirts. She was a nasty freckled little thing. She threw a worm at me once."

"But she's grown up now, and very pretty. I'm sure she won't throw any more worms! Look! You surely can't just let an old chum sit all alone like that!"

"But poets don't dance, you know!"

"Hmm... I understand Mr. Coleridge was very fond of dancing," said Imogen mendaciously. "He said it stirred his creative juices."

"Really?" The poet was intrigued. "I can see how it might. Oh, very well, I'll ask her."

He wandered downstairs and Imogen was glad to see him make his bow to the young woman in question. The pair of them fell into what seemed to be easy conversation, and when the next dance began, Lord Fairclough led his old friend onto the floor with every appearance of pleasure.

"Very well done, Imogen!" said Adrian Brody in his soft burr. "But when will you start taking a turn on the floor yourself? I'd be happy to lead you, me darlin'."

"Not yet, Adrian," she replied. "Perhaps in a month or so."

"Then let it not be more," responded her friend. "You know Fordyce would not be liking you to be in mourning for so long!"

Imogen agreed that he would not, but reflected that it had, in fact, been very convenient to wear mourning. On the one hand, young bucks who might otherwise have ogled her or pestered her to dance were put off by her weeds, and other people were inclined to take a widow more seriously than someone they perceived as a green girl. For a woman engaged in business, it had been very useful indeed, and she was sure Fordyce would understand that.

Chapter Twelve

If anyone had asked her, Imogen would have said that her life was complete. She was head of her own household. She controlled her own finances and with her absorbing interest in new industrial development had even been able to improve them. She had family and friends around her. After her interlude with the Duke of Sarisbury, however, she had to admit to herself that in spite of her formal dismissal of him, he was almost constantly in her thoughts. What she had told him was absolutely true: his way of life was anathema to her and she would never be counted amongst his paramours. Nonetheless, of all the men she had ever met, and she begged Fordyce's forgiveness here, he was the most fascinating. When he kissed her, he was almost irresistible.

However, about a week later, she received by the morning post a note from Mr. Carter that temporarily chased all other thoughts from her mind. It read:

> *Cheapside, London.*
> *My dear Mrs. Mainwaring,*
>
> *I trust this letter finds you happy and in good health, and I hope that your new residence in London is in every way satisfactory.*

You asked me to keep you informed of any new investment opportunities, and I believe I have one that is interesting. I know you are aware of the rapid development of the railways. One of the latest proposals is for railway lines that run direct from city to city, as the crow flies, so to speak. This is clearly the fastest and cheapest option and appears eminently sensible.

The case in point is a proposal for a London to Deal direct rail. If you are not familiar with Deal, it is an ancient port in Kent on the south-east coast, a few miles east of Dover. It has for many years enjoyed a profitable shipping business with the Continent. In previous times it was known for smuggling, but that need not concern us now. Even during the troubled years of Napoleon there was little interruption in this commerce, and it is to the boatmen of Deal that we owed most of the news that arrived from the Continent. Clearly, with the revolts in France at last (dare we hope?) at an end, and with a direct rail link to London, such trade will only increase.

I believe I mentioned to you that the Government Bonds, in which a large proportion of your fortune is invested, are now only yielding 4%. It happens that a number of them become due this quarter and would provide us with a handsome sum to invest, something in the region of ten thousand pounds.

I await your instructions on the matter, but I urge you to act quite quickly, as the available shares are selling fast.

In anticipation, I am your devoted servant,
Martin Carter.

Imogen sat for a minute with the letter in her lap, staring into space as she tried to envisage the route a direct train from London to Deal might take. Apart from the trip she had taken to Whitstable, which went in the general direction of Deal, she was not familiar with that part of the country. But as a child she had been made to study a book entitled *The Geographical Magazine* which contained maps and descriptions of the various parts of Britain. She tried to remember what it said about Kent. She had never been very interested in British geography, and as a young person had never travelled much outside Nottinghamshire and the surrounding counties, so her memories were very hazy.

The one thing she did remember was the term *The Weald of Kent*, though what exactly it was escaped her. She determined to go to a library that afternoon and see if she could find a detailed map of the county. In the meantime, she penned a hasty note to Mr. Carter asking him to refrain from any share purchase in the proposed rail line until she could do further investigation. If it meant she lost the opportunity, so be it, but she would not risk any placement until she knew more.

That afternoon she went to the Minerva Press Circulating Library and found a volume of detailed county maps. In front of the window of the establishment there was a large table with benches provided for readers of volumes too big to hold, so she laid it out there and opened it to the page devoted to Kent. She saw that the county bordered the Thames and the North Sea to the north, and the English Channel to the south. The chalk ridge of the North Downs ran west to east through the county, petering out as it went further east. North of the Downs was the marshland of the Thames estuary and south of them the Weald, which Imogen now saw was a rolling woodland area. The River Medway created a valley more or less north to south, and the Stour ran east to west through the Weald. A direct rail line from London to Deal would therefore have to cross the Medway, traverse the rolling wooded hills of the Weald, and cross the Stour before descending into the town. The difficulty and cost of the engineering required would be enormous, if it could be achieved at all.

As she sat in rapt attention, her eyes on the book in front of her but her brain whirring, a well-known voice suddenly brought her out of her reverie.

"My dear Mrs. Mainwaring! I thought it was you staring at that enormous volume," said the Duke of Sarisbury. "I was walking by and happened to glance in. What on earth are you doing studying…," he bent over the page "… Kent. Don't tell me you are moving there to get away from me. Unnecessary, I assure you."

She had instinctively looked up with a smile at the sound of his voice, then wished she had not, for the expression in his eyes disturbed her. She hoped he was not going to refer to their meeting at Almack's.

"Don't be ridiculous," she answered tartly, trying to depress any familiarity. "I'm not moving to Kent. I'm studying the topography to see if a rail line directly across it is feasible. On the whole I think not. There are wide rivers, forests and hills to contend with."

"Good God, is that what you spend your time doing? Studying railway lines and geography books? I hadn't realized you were such a bluestocking. Does your black-haired bodyguard know about this?"

"Adrian Brody is not my bodyguard. He is a good friend. And yes, he knows I like to study things. In this case, the feasibility of a direct line to Deal. There are share options on the market to finance it, which apparently a number of people have already bought. It has been suggested that I might do the same, but I don't like the look of it."

"Imogen, you never cease to amaze me," said Ivo, "I knew Mainwaring was a pretty warm man, but I didn't realize you were his business adviser."

"I wasn't. I knew nothing about it until after his death, after I came back from Lausanne, in fact. I was bored and started reading about it. Then I found I had a knack for investments. I don't sew, paint or play the pianoforte, but, though I know it's unladylike to mention it, I can make money."

"Then we should suit perfectly!" laughed the Duke. "You only know how to make money and I only know how to spend it! But now you mention this direct line thing, I remember hearing something about it in the club the other day. A couple of chaps encouraging a third to invest. They even tried to speak to me, but I had to tell them I don't know a share from a sandcastle. Put them onto my man of business. He handles all that for me. I only see him when I have to sign something."

"Then you are very foolish. You'd better make sure he hasn't put any money into this scheme. I am going down to Kent to look around, but I'm almost sure it is not a good investment."

"Going to Kent? Good God, that's taking your studies to extremes! I'd better come with you. You definitely need me to protect you. They're all smugglers and pirates down there, and they speak in such a dialect you can't understand a word!"

"As I've told you before, the only person I need protection from is you. You are most certainly not accompanying me. I will go nowhere in your company. Mr. Brody will come."

"But how can I convince you my offer is made with the purest of motives? We would only be together during the day, and I won't even try to kiss you again, unless you throw yourself at me again." The Duke raised his mobile eyebrows. "Damme, I would be jealous of this Brody if I didn't have the distinct impression…," he broke off and resumed in a different tone, "So, once again I am to be rejected. It's a good thing I know my own worth or I would be driven to despair."

Imogen bit her lip, then said, "On that topic, I must make you an apology. I was very rude to you the other day at Almack's. I should not have said what I did. I'm very sorry."

"You mean about Mainwaring being twice the man I am? Don't apologize. You are probably right, at least, to judge from the woman he got to marry him."

And with that, he gave her a brief bow, picked up his cane to his hat, and left the library.

Imogen closed the book and mechanically returned it to the shelves, thinking about the Duke's last remark and trying to ignore the emotional disturbance being with him always caused. Then she gave herself a shake. Enough! Back to business: she would have to go into Kent. Before leaving the library, she bought a little book entitled *Travelers' Kent: A Guide for the Discriminating,* which provided essential information about roads, inns, and sites to visit. Thus armed, she went home to plan her trip.

Adrian Brody was quite prepared to accompany her, and her aunt, who had previously tried to prevent her from undertaking what she considered dangerous trips, accepted the plan easily enough. The first part of the trip was a repeat of the one she had made to Whitstable, except this time they would stay overnight in Maidstone. Consulting her tour guide, Imogen wrote to the White Rabbit Inn to bespeak rooms and stabling there. The next day they would leave early so as to lunch in Canterbury and give the horses a good rest before the final push into Deal. To save time, they would not stay in the town itself, as they had before, but on the outskirts at the toll gate. The Old Gate Inn was the best choice. Accordingly, she wrote to bespeak rooms and stabling. In Deal they would lodge at the Swan Inn, a well-known posting house with stabling for twenty horses. Two days should be enough there.

They left two days later. It was an arduous trip. The White Rabbit Inn in Maidstone had been built as an officers' barracks in the late eighteenth century and offered little in the way of luxury, but it was clean and quiet, and the food, while simple, was plentiful. The Old Gate Inn in Canterbury, in contrast, offered timbered rooms and feather beds but was extremely noisy, with a constant passage of coaches and carriages blowing their horns to summon the toll man, so that the hoped-for rest was practically impossible.

After Canterbury, the road to Deal became less frequented and more difficult. It was only eighteen miles, but seemed much longer. It rolled up and down sometimes through thick woods and sometimes through sandy plains. To relieve the horses, they walked part of the way, so it was a very weary group that descended on The Swan in Deal. They ate a belated supper and collapsed into bed.

The first day of their stay in Deal, they walked down to the port and looked back at the town. It was clear that no work had as yet begun on the proposed rail line. The town sloped upwards towards the hills behind it, though not dramatically so, nothing like the white cliffs at Dover that Imogen had seen travelling to and from the Continent. However, as she had learned from her trip to Whitstable, anything more than a slight incline would necessitate stationary steam engines, as the locomotives were not powerful enough to pull up slopes unaided.

Much would depend upon the engineer's report. The chief problem was crossing the wide Medway and then the Weald with its woods and rolling terrain. Water would have to be pumped from either the Medway or the Stour, or both, to provision the tanks along such a long route. All in all, while a direct line might be possible, it would be very difficult and expensive and she considered nothing much would be gained. The line could just as easily follow the road to Canterbury and then to Deal. It would be cheaper and also have the advantage of taking in both towns.

It was the activity along the shore itself that really opened her eyes. Deal had no real port. Its maritime fame came from the sheltered area between the shore and the Goodwin Sands. This was a natural breakwater four miles offshore, invisible at low tide but a treacherous invisible quicksand when the tide was in. The area between the Sands and the shore provided safe anchorage for boats waiting to be provisioned before they continued their journey to London and further up the east coast, or west to Southampton and beyond, or across the Channel.

The landlord of the inn had told them that Deal boatmen had traditionally made their living by *hovelling* or carrying goods and provisions in *luggers* to the large boats anchored there. They also acted as pilots for boats finding their way around this tricky passage and salvaged boats that quite often foundered there. By Charter they also had the right to trade across the Channel.

During the time of the Napoleonic Wars, hovelling had reached its zenith, with over 400 ships of the British Navy being stationed there

However, it seemed that with peacetime, work had dropped off very significantly. Imogen and Adrian could see some larger boats at anchor out beyond the shore, but most of the *luggers* used for provisioning them lay on the steeply sloping shingle beach, in poor condition and clearly not in constant use. Where was the bustling port that was to provide goods for railway transport? They walked down to the beach and talked to one boatman sitting on an upturned barrel smoking a pipe.

"Aye," he said, "sixteen yar ago oi 'ad seven boats, now oi got but one and she be an old 'un."

They spent about an hour on the beach looking out at the sea without observing a great deal of activity among the boats laid up there. Adrian took out his sketch pad and used the time drawing the picturesque scene, which while artistically satisfactory, from a business point of view was disappointing.

They spent the rest of the day exploring the ancient town of Deal, with its narrow streets overhung with medieval buildings. The town was mentioned in the Domesday Book and had been the site of various battles between pretenders to the English throne and foreign invaders, notably the French. The town's less salubrious history, according to the guide book, was, as the Duke had said, to do with the smuggling that took place along the coast. In January 1794 the then Prime Minister, William Pitt the Younger, believing that their wholesale smuggling had a negative effect on the Exchequer, had tried to put an end to it by burning the boats on the beach when they had been laid up out of the weather. But these efforts had been largely forgotten and the trade continued, especially since the end of the valid work brought in by the Napoleonic era. It was said that hardly an inn between the Kentish coast and London paid duty on the casks that lay in their cellars. After dinner in the inn that evening, Mr. Brody commented on the very excellent brandy he was served, and drank an ironic toast to William Pitt.

The following day, having achieved the purpose of the trip, they hired a hack to take them sightseeing to various sites out of town mentioned by the guide book. They trotted along the beach road to Walmer, where Julius Caesar was said to have landed, perhaps even twice. Then they went up to Walmer Castle, originally built as a fort in 1539. It was now the official residence of the Warden of the Cinque Ports. The Warden and his family were from home, but the housekeeper showed them over the Castle.

Outside, it was very impressive, with crenelated towers accessed by a bridge over the moat, but the interior was a fairly ordinary family home. Imogen confidingly whispered to Adrian that she was glad she did not have to pay the coal bills or mount the stone staircases on a daily basis. However, she agreed that the fine view over the sea and shore from the parapet was worth the climb.

The exhausted party arrived back in London almost a week after their departure, and one of the first things Imogen did after a good night's sleep, thankfully unbroken by the shouts of ostlers or the blowing of the tin horn, was to read the accumulation of newspapers on her desk. To her surprise, a headline from two days previously read:

Direct Rail to Deal. Questions Asked.

The article said that there were rumors in the City about the viability of the proposed direct rail link between London and the port of Deal, for which a large number of shares had already been sold. A meeting to which all interested parties were invited was scheduled in two days. She would be there.

Chapter Thirteen

When the Duke of Sarisbury left Imogen in the Minerva Library, he made his leisurely way to his club, thoughtfully swinging his cane. Walking in, he saw a couple of the men who had proposed the London-Deal railway investment a few days before.

"I say, Whitmore," he addressed a portly, white haired gentleman. "You remember that London to Deal train business you were talking about?"

"Certainly, Sarisbury, I just bought more shares today. Apparently they've already laid fifteen miles of track. You'd better hurry—price is going up and up."

"Hmm…," his Grace appeared to ponder. "Can't say I know Kent well, wild place full of smugglers, I hear, but is the topography suited to railway lines, the Weald and so on?"

"The top-what?"

" -ography. Topography. Study of how the land lies, so to speak," replied the Duke, in an off-hand manner and beginning to move off. "But you've seen the engineering report, so you know better than me. Anyone knows better than me, come to that."

"Engineering report? What report?"

"I don't know, but I'm sure there is one. But as I say, don't ask me. I know nothing of the matter."

This was not, of course, wholly true. His Grace knew enough to proceed straight to the Reading Room and write a note to his man of business instructing him to sell immediately whatever shares he might have bought in the National and International Railway, Inc. He had heard it was unfeasible.

Watching the Duke make his languid way into the Reading Room, Lord Whitmore turned to his companion. "Can never tell if the man's a fool or not," he remarked.

"I think he's a lot more canny than he lets on," said his friend. "What's this business about an engineering report? Have you seen one?"

"Not I! I got the tip from old Dicky Grimstone. He may have seen it. He'll probably be in later, we can ask him."

But when Mr. Grimstone came in, he said that he had heard about the investment from Charlie Pickering and had never seen an engineering report. And so it went on. Everyone had heard about it from someone else and that someone else from someone else. No one had ever seen an engineering report. In a matter of days, questions were being asked all around the clubs and in the city. The Duke's man had meanwhile quietly sold the shares he had previously acquired, and since the price had gone up, he made a tidy profit.

When he reported this to his Grace, the Duke laughed out loud. "Wait till I tell her!" he said, a pronouncement that mystified his listener.

Adrian Brody had agreed to accompany Imogen to the meeting, but at the last minute had been forced to send a note saying he had a putrid sore throat and could not come. Nothing daunted, Imogen decided to go alone. A little ahead of the appointed hour, she entered the offices in Fleet Street that bore the promising title of *National and International Railways Inc.* She had put on what she thought the most severe of her semi-mourning gowns in pale lilac superfine wool. Over a fairly full skirt that nevertheless followed the shape of her hips, a military style jacket with a row of smart black buttons down the front fitted closely over her bosom and to her trim waist. The stand-up collar and turned-back sleeves were edged in black braid. Her hat, with its black feather that fell over the brim at the back, matched the gown, and as usual she wore her black lace cap and gloves. She was obviously a widow, but a very pretty one. An usher came to her, his brow furrowed, asking if she was looking for someone.

"No," she replied, holding her head high. "I am here on my own account. The article in *The Times* said the meeting was for all interested parties. I am an interested party."

"Well… er… this is most irregular," said the usher, embarrassed. "We do not usually expect ladies at these things. No arrangements have been made."

"I need no special arrangements," replied Imogen. "I am here to listen, like everyone else."

"I… er… I shall have to ask Mr. Farah, our Director," murmured the usher. "If you would be so kind as to wait a few minutes."

Once he had left, the way was clear into the meeting room and Imogen walked boldly in. It was a large room with a long table in the center surrounded by chairs for about forty people. All around the walls were extra seats. Men were standing around in small groups, talking. All conversation gradually ceased as Imogen made her way to the middle of the table and sat down.

Almost at once, a short man with dark oiled hair came to her and, with a strained smile, bowed and said, "Madame, allow me to introduce myself. I am David Farah, Director of National and International Railways. It is always a pleasure to see one of the fairer sex, especially, if I may say, one as lovely as yourself, but I fear you have come to the wrong place. Perhaps your... husband is waiting for you elsewhere?"

"I have no husband," said Imogen coldly in a clear, carrying voice. "And if this is where the proposed direct rail from London to Deal will be discussed, I am in the right place."

"But, Madame, we have no accommodations for ladies," said Mr. Farah, in a voice one might have used for the mentally defective. "I fear you will not be comfortable here."

"As I have already told your man, I need no accommodations. Tell me at once, Mr. Farah," said Imogen, fixing him with a stare, "are women not permitted to invest in your... venture?"

"But of course they are, Madame" the Director replied placatingly. "But generally your affairs would be managed by a... gentleman."

"I have neither husband nor gentleman to manage my affairs for me, and I need none. If you have nothing more to say, please leave me in peace. I'm sure you have better things to do in preparation for this meeting."

"That's right, Farah," said a familiar voice, "leave Mrs. Mainwaring in peace. She has as much right to hear what you have to say as the rest of us."

The Duke of Sarisbury had entered the room and, like everyone else, had heard their exchange. He now bowed to Imogen, murmured with a smile, "If you permit," and sat down next to her. She turned and gave him a nod of thanks, but other than that, did not acknowledge him. She did not want to appear intimate with him with so many people watching. But she could feel his broad shoulders and arms next to hers, and the knowledge of his closeness heightened all her senses. She looked down, drew from her reticule the notes she had made and pretended to read them. Mr. Farah gave up on trying to remove this woman, championed as she was by the Duke, but he could not imagine what she was doing there. He was to find out.

In a few minutes the usher called, "Take your seats, gentlemen, please," and the assembled company either found places at the table, or around the walls. Mr. Farah walked importantly to the head of the table and addressed them.

"I take it as a mark of confidence in National and International Railways that so many of you have come here today to hear of the progress we are making in our latest venture, the direct rail line between London and Deal, in Kent. As you know, the town of Deal has for many years been an important point of importation and exportation for products to and from the Continent."

Here he went into a series of statistics about the hundredweights of ships in the port, and the volume of trade in pecks, bushels, and barrels. Having seen the lack of activity on the beach the week before Imogen knew this was a falsehood. The statistics must date from fifteen to twenty years earlier.

Mr. Farah continued. "I am therefore very happy to report that ground has already been broken in the construction of our direct railway link to that bustling port and we expect completion before the middle of next year."

There was a relieved mutter around the room as the men turned to each other and nodded. This came to an abrupt halt as the clear voice of Imogen was heard. She had stood up and was looking straight at the Director.

"May I ask you, Mr. Farah, where ground has been broken to construct this railway?"

"Why, Madam, in the town of Deal, of course."

"And from what date are the statistics of imported and exported goods that you have just quoted?"

"Hmm… just one moment, Madam. Please allow me to verify that information." He riffled through a number of papers and finally peered at one page through a pince-nez. "That would be 1829, Madam, last year, in fact."

"And, finally, may I ask the nature of the terrain that the railway will traverse?"

"The railway will proceed straight across the county in a southeasterly direction."

"In view of the answers you have given, Mr. Farah," pronounced Imogen clearly, "I must accuse you of misleading this assembly." There was a collective gasp. Imogen continued as if she had not heard it. "It would no doubt surprise you to learn that I spent last week travelling to Deal. The port of Deal is in fact a simple shoreline which is protected by a ten-mile sand bank, providing sheltered anchorage and a re-provisioning stop for vessels on their way east up to the Thames estuary and London, west to Southampton or across the Channel. During the wars with Bonaparte there was indeed a thriving business there, with upwards of four hundred Navy boats at anchor needed constant re-provisioning. But with the departure of the Royal Navy, those days are over. These days there are far fewer boats at anchor in the sheltered channel and many of the boats that were once used to service them now lie rotting and unused on the beach. There is very little merchandise off-loaded at Deal. I can also tell you that traversing the county in a straight line is impracticable. One would have to cross the wide Medway river, then the Weald, a rolling, forested and hillocked area. It is for that reason that all road traffic currently goes via Canterbury. The town of Deal itself lies on an incline from the hills behind it to a steep pebble beach. Furthermore, there is no sign anywhere of any construction of a railway. But I presume an engineering report has been done, and I must therefore ask you to show this assembly this report which will no doubt lay out the work required to cross this terrain." She sat down.

The other people in the room took up the line. "The engineering report. Let us see the engineering report. Where is the engineering report?" The demand rose to a crescendo. Mr. Farah raised both his hands and cried, "Gentlemen, Gentlemen... and Madam, please, please! Allow me to step out of the room and I will bring back the report you are asking for." He left the room at a rapid walk that broke into a trot as he got to the door. People who had half risen sat down again in their seats, talking urgently to their neighbors. Imogen could hear *Who is she?* and *Mrs. Mainwaring* and *old Fordy Mainwaring's widow* and *what if she's right?* being passed from mouth to mouth. She was very uncomfortable and only the solid mass of the Duke of Sarisbury next to her kept her still in her seat.

Minutes passed, five, ten, fifteen. Finally, one of the men nearest the door cried, "I'll fetch the wretched fellow. Let's put an end to this!" He left the room and returned a few minutes later. "The damned villain has gone! Both him and that usher fellow. Disappeared! Vanished!"

There was an immediate uproar. A babble of voices. "Where's he gone?" "What does this mean?" "It's a damned fraud!" "How do I get my money back?"

The Duke touched Imogen's sleeve. "Come along, Imogen. We're best out of this." He took her arm and firmly led her through the throng that was beginning to crowd through the door and onto the street. Several tried to stop her with questions, but, ignoring them, he propelled her forward.

"Where's your carriage?" he said.

"Just around the corner. I told my driver to meet me there." He walked her quickly to her carriage, helped her in and told the driver to wait while he gave instructions to his tiger to follow them in his phaeton. He was soon back and they set off at a trot for Mayfair.

The Duke sat in one corner, his long legs stretched out across the floor of the carriage, regarding her with a look of amusement in his eyes. Her bosom was rising and falling rapidly with both the exertion of almost running from the assembly and from her anxiety at the situation. She looked absurdly youthful.

He waited until she had calmed a little before saying casually, "You know, Imogen, it seems that things traditionally come in threes: the three little pigs, the three wise men, the three wishes of Aladdin... I'm sure there are many others. Therefore," and he slid down the banquette towards her, "you owe me another kiss."

He put one arm around her waist and with his other hand turned her face up to his. Before she could say or do anything, he kissed her long and firmly, as he had twice before, his tongue this time making a further foray into her mouth. She was too startled to struggle and soon too much engaged by the kiss to wish to. Her heart, which had just ceased to beat so fast, leaped up again and she felt herself entirely overtaken. After what seemed both an age and a minute, his lips left hers and she came to her senses. Placing her palms flat against his broad chest, she pushed him away.

"No, Ivo, no! You cannot keep kissing me like this!" she cried.

"Why not, when we both enjoy it so much?" He smiled down at her.

"Because... because it's just not right!"

"But if you would accept my offer and live under my protection, I would have every right. And you need the protection, Imogen! You can't carry on like you did today without someone behind you. Where's that damned Brady?"

"Mr. Brody," she emphasized the name, "is indisposed and I had to come alone. I didn't plan it that way. I don't need your protection and I don't want it. Stop smiling at me like that. And stop kissing me!"

"I will not undertake to stop kissing you, in fact I shall kiss you every chance I get. You should be happy. You like it, don't try to deny it."

Imogen sighed. "Very well, I won't deny it. I do like it, heaven knows why, since I don't like you. Or at least, I don't like the type of man you are. But just because one likes something that doesn't mean one should have it all the time. I am very fond of lemon cream, but I don't eat it every day."

"That is definitely where we differ. If I like a thing I want it every day. I like you very much, and I want you every day. You say you don't like the type of man I am, but you haven't given me a chance. If you had never tasted lemon cream, you wouldn't know you liked it so much. Likewise with me. Give me a try! I promise you, I'm even better than lemon cream."

"Don't be ridiculous! No, no and no! And do not ask me again. The answer will always be no! Thank you for helping me today, though I'm sure I could have managed on my own." Here she was not being entirely truthful, as his strong presence had been a decided comfort to her, and she knew it. Nevertheless, she continued, "Contrary to the opinion of Society, a woman does not always need a man. I am in the lucky position of being very able to do without one. Why would I give up my independence to come under the protection, as you call it, of someone like you? How long does your protection last? A couple of weeks? A month? Then what? Do I seek the protection of someone else? And then someone else after that? Where does it end? When I'm too old and ugly for anyone to want to protect me, just at the point in my life when I may actually need it? Don't you see that what you're offering is no gift? It is ruin! Not financial, perhaps, but personal. A woman who has enjoyed so much protection must almost inevitably end up alone and miserable, her reputation ruined! Even you must see that!"

The Duke made a flippant remark, but in truth he was taken aback. He had never thought about it before, and he could see that much of what she said was right. Of course, there were wealthy society women who were known to have entertained a series of lovers and who were still accepted in their own right. But if they had no fortune, it must be as Imogen had described. Of course, if what one heard was true, she herself was possessed of a substantial fortune, so she need never fear. Then again, in offering a carte blanche to her, he had had no thought of what might happen afterwards. To his surprise, the idea that she might subsequently fall into someone else's bed dismayed him. He was still pondering this when the carriage drew up in front of her residence.

"I won't ask you in," said Imogen, gathering up her reticule, "as I really much prefer my aunt not to know that we are acquainted. I'm sure you understand."

"Of course." The Duke smiled. "I am debauched. I know. Let me help you down, however."

He leaped from his side of the carriage and went around to the other side as the driver was putting down the steps for his mistress. He took Imogen's hand, turned it over and kissed the palm.

"I don't promise not to importune you anymore," he said seriously. "but I shall think about what you said. And by the way, thank you. I sold my shares after our meeting in the library and I made a tidy profit. My man of business no doubt considers me a genius! Goodbye, my dear."

He put his hat on his head, touched the top of his cane to it, and walked swiftly to his phaeton, waiting a few yards down the street. Imogen went thoughtfully indoors. He had never called her *my dear* before. Somehow, it touched her heart more than all his flattering speeches had ever done.

Chapter Fourteen

It was not long before the abortive meeting and the disappearance of the principals of National and International Railways, Inc. was widely known. *The Times* reported on it the next day:

> *A meeting at the offices of National and International Railways, Inc. ended in chaos yesterday as a Mrs. Mannering refuted the assertions made by the Director David Farah and called for an engineering report. Under the guise of leaving the meeting to obtain this report, Mr. Farah and his colleague, known only as Adam, apparently left the premises and could be found nowhere in the City. The share price, which started the day at 19s 15d fell precipitously as soon as this was known. This morning it stood at 5s 2d. Unhappy investors are calling for an official investigation into Mr. Farah's business practices.*

Imogen could have wished her name had not been mentioned, but since it was misspelled, perhaps no one would identify her by it. Later in the day she received a note from Mr. Carter, congratulating her on her foresight in not purchasing the shares he had suggested. The following weeks saw more newspaper reports in which Mr. Farah was discovered to have perpetrated fraud on a number of other occasions, notably in America where he went variously by the names of Farrish, Parrah and Parrish. He and his co-conspirator were nowhere to be found and speculation was rife that they had escaped to the Continent.

Imogen stayed close to home, not wishing to be embroiled in any of the turmoil. She sent her excuses to all dinner invitations, went to no routs or balls, and contented herself with her aunt's small card parties. At the same time, she decided that she could now put off her black gloves altogether. It had been a full year since Fordyce's death. She therefore put away her purples and lilacs and went back with relief to her normal clothes. In the year she had been in mourning, the styles had not changed too much. Nevertheless, one place she did go was to her *modiste* to place orders for new gowns in the greens, ambers, and reds she had so missed.

She was not, however, able to escape the attentions of the young Lord Fairclough. He had discovered her address and not a day passed without his appearing there, bringing posies, or more often, a piece of verse, which he would hand to her, beautifully lettered in a scroll tied with ribbon. One such, which nearly made her laugh out loud, ran:

Bright Star! O Imogen!
Why dost thou shine
On all the world but I?
O would that thou wert in mine arms,
And not above so high!
I lie in tears upon mine couch
With Death mine only friend.
For if thou refuse all I can give,
My life will surely end.

So put thy kiss upon my brow
And say you will be mine.
For in heaven above, of all the stars
For me, none but thee doth shine.

"My dear Lord Fairclough, Desmond!" she said, concentrating on the serious aspect of the poem and trying to keep a straight face. I cannot tell you how it disturbs me to hear you talk of your death! Pray, do not make me think of it!"

"But Imogen," he cried, "Indeed I cannot live without you. I swear I will do myself an injury if you do not run away with me!"

"You know I cannot do that. Think how horrified all the people who love us will be! Your mother, my aunt, your sisters! I am persuaded they would never forgive me!"

"What do I care for them?" protested the poet. "My muse needs you. Without you, I am nothing!"

In the end, he would either rush from the house in a desperate frenzy, or Imogen would persuade him to take her to the park in his curricle, where the gold of the autumn, and then, as the season progressed, the dying and falling leaves, seemed exactly suited to his elegiac mood. To keep him from the topic of marriage and running away, she would encourage him to make such observations of nature that might best be turned into a poetic image. In this way she was responsible for one of his slightly more felicitous attempts, which was actually published in the *London Gazette*:

The image of the leaves I see
First gold then deadly brown,
Upon my heart their mark do make
When my mistress' brow doth frown.
I, like them, in her smile am gold,

But dead, when refusal she returns.
For without her love, my autumn love
Is fire, consuming what it burns.

Unfortunately, he entitled this oeuvre For *Imogen in the Park*, and since she had been seen there in his company quite frequently, the publication gave rise to ribald remarks from the gentlemen of the *ton* and sighing sympathy from the maidens. In any case, Lord Fairclough's reputation soared and he enjoyed a popularity amongst the ladies he had never known before.

One of the witnesses to their fairly frequent rides in the park was the Duke of Sarisbury. It seemed to Imogen that they saw him there on nearly every occasion. He would lightly touch his cane to his hat as he swept by in his high perch phaeton, but he never engaged her in any other way. She struggled with herself to stop her heart from lifting every time she saw him, and felt unaccountably dejected when she did not.

A person who appeared a great deal more concerned about this relationship than the Duke was Lord Fairclough's mother. One morning a week or so after the publication of the poem, Imogen was astonished by her butler coming into her office, bearing a card on a salver, to announce that Lady Fairclough had asked to see her and was waiting in the drawing room. She knew from what her suitor had told her that his mother rarely came to London, preferring to live quietly at their country estate. She entered to find a tall, thin lady dressed well, but in the style of perhaps five years before, standing in front of the fire.

"Lady Fairclough! This is a pleasant surprise! I had no idea you were in London, or I would have...."

Before she could finish her sentence, the lady came towards her with outstretched arms crying in throbbing accents, "I must beg you, dear Mrs. Mainwaring, to release my child!"

"Whatever can you mean, Lady Fairclough?" cried Imogen in return. "Release him? I am not holding him! Indeed, it is quite the reverse! He pursues me and threatens to harm himself if I will not receive him. I assure you, it is the last thing I desire!"

"But I've been told you ride with him in the park and entertain him here in your home."

"He is never here without my aunt as chaperone and I make him take me up in his curricle precisely to get him out of my house. In the park he cannot make such a cake of himself."

"But he says you are his Muse and he will never rest until you become his wife! Now I see how pretty and young-looking you are, I understand how he can have fallen in love with you. But you must see, it is impossible! He is only twenty and you must be... several years older. And you are childless widow. The succession must be maintained, you know, and an older woman who was married before and has no child...." Her voice tailed off, but her meaning was clear. A barren older widow was no wife for the Fairclough heir.

"I assure you, Lady Fairclough, I have no thoughts at all of becoming your son's wife. I agree, I'm much too old for him. It's out of the question." Then, in desperation for a convincing argument, "Besides, my affections are engaged elsewhere."

This did the trick. At once, Lady Fairclough relaxed.

"Oh, my dear! I cannot say how happy I am to hear it. But how is it you have not told him this?"

"I do not want to make him unhappy! He threatens such awful things. Really, Lady Fairclough, if you could but send him away for a time. He is not happy at Oxford, indeed, he must already be in trouble there for missing nearly this whole term. Couldn't you send him to Greece for the winter to see the ruins and the statues? Tell him that all the great poets have been inspired by them. I'm sure he'll go."

"What a happy thought!" cried the fond Mama. "The very thing! I've no doubt he will be extremely unhappy when I tell him your affections are engaged elsewhere, so he may indeed be induced to leave the country for a spell. I cannot tell you what relief you have brought to a mother's heart!"

"I too am glad we have settled this between us. Please won't you have a cup of tea with my aunt and me before you go?" She rang the bell for tea and asked the butler to see if Aunt Dorothea was free.

The three ladies sat companionably talking of this and that for almost another hour, until Lady Fairclough gasped at the clock and took her leave. Imogen excused herself and walked thoughtfully back to her study. In the time remaining before the bell rang for luncheon she wanted to look at a plan she had been forming since her return from Deal.

While it was true that Mr. Farah's proposal had lacked merit, and indeed had been a fraud from the start, it was also true that the country was in need of a train line to the south coast. Dover was a better choice than Deal as this port was the surest link to the Continent, and now, with peace in France, travel there must increase. The road there was quite good but for people who had not the means to ride in their own carriage, the post coach was slow, even though quite often instead of stopping, the mail was simply thrown down, and it was uncomfortable, being usually filled to capacity.

She decided to go back to the library to look at the county map. Her railway would almost certainly not be a direct line, but would follow the old roads, some of them the old Roman roads which were certainly the easiest, if not the most direct. If all went well, she could open a branch line to Canterbury, and the other larger cities in Kent. She wrote a note to Mr. Carter informing him of her intentions and asking him for advice on how to proceed.

She had just finished this when there was another interruption. This time her butler informed her that Lord Fairclough was asking for her. With great misgivings she went out into the hall to greet him and was surprised to find that he was, for once, quite cheerful. It became clear that he had not seen his mother. She had gone out before he was up and he had lunched with friends. Imogen was relieved. She did not think she could bear recriminations from two members of the same family in one day. He invited her to ride in the park, and since the afternoon was fine and she had not been outside all day, she accepted.

"Just give me a few minutes to put on my walking dress," she said. "I can't go out in this." She was wearing a pale green silk dress with delicate white embroidered flowers on the skirt, clearly inappropriate for riding out, so the young lord made no demur. She appeared about twenty minutes later in a green and grey herringbone superfine wool walking dress with a matching grey pelisse and gloves, and a green poke bonnet with a grey feather sweeping back from the crown. The color enhanced her eyes and her black curls clustered prettily around her face. She looked lovely.

Lord Fairclough took her on his arm and helped her into his curricle which was waiting outside. No groom stood with the horse. It was being held instead by an urchin who eagerly caught the coin tossed by his lordship and then ran off. Imogen thought this a little strange, but since her suitor was given to odd starts, she quickly forgot about it. They trotted towards the park, which lay not far from her home, and began their normal perambulation. Imogen tried to draw his lordship's attention to the foliage, now in its last stages of life, and to the faded colors and stiff attitudes of the few dried-out flowers still left in the beds, but he seemed strangely uninterested. All at once, he drew the curricle into a sheltered area and stopped. Imogen thought he was going to try to kiss her and prepared to fight him off, but to her surprise, he jumped down from the vehicle, came to her side and said,

"May I ask you to descend for a minute please, Mrs. Mainwaring?"

"Why?" she queried, reasonably enough.

"There's... er... something I want to show you. A bird's nest," he said, not altogether convincingly.

"A bird's nest? It must have blown down from the trees. There are no birds in it, surely, at this time of the year?"

She allowed herself to be swung from the curricle. As soon as her feet were on the ground, Lord Fairclough took her around the waist and urged her forward through the bushes. Too surprised to resist at first, Imogen only became alarmed when she saw a coach and four waiting on the other side of the bushes on the perimeter road of the park. Gripping her more tightly still, Lord Fairclough more or less pushed her towards it.

"No! No! My lord! Desmond! What on earth are you about!" she cried. "Let me go! No! No!"

The Duke of Sarisbury had come to the park that fine afternoon, thinking he might catch a glimpse of Imogen with her young suitor. He had heard in the clubs that the beautiful widow was being courted by the younger man, and, like the rest, had laughed over the poem in the *Gazette*. Since her outpouring to him in the carriage after the Farah débacle, he had found her almost constantly his thoughts. He did not really think that she would seriously consider marriage to Fairclough, but she had so vehemently criticized his profligate lifestyle that he wondered whether an inexperienced boy might hold some attraction for her.

He suddenly saw what he knew to be Fairclough's curricle partially hidden by bushes, the fine chestnut left cropping at the grass border. The Duke immediately drew to a halt and ordered his tiger to walk the bays, while he took long strides over to the abandoned horse, rubbed its nose and said softly,

"Now where's he gone and what's he doing, eh?"

The horse snickered in his ear but otherwise gave no answer. None was needed, for at that moment the Duke heard Imogen's cry. Within seconds he had pushed through the bushes and was abreast of Lord Fairclough as he tried to force her into the coach.

"When a lady says no, she means no, my boy," he said agreeably, taking Lord Fairclough by the scruff of the neck. "In my day they taught us that at Eton, but it seems standards have sadly dropped."

Without appearing to make the slightest effort, he lifted the younger man off his feet and dropped him to the ground an arm's length away.

"Come, Mrs. Mainwaring," he continued, almost in the same breath, "I fear there has been a misunderstanding. Allow me to take you home." He put her hand on his arm and patted it. "Lord Fairclough has made a mistake."

He turned to the coach driver. "Here's for your pains," he said, throwing a gold coin. "Your services are no longer required. Be off."

Lord Fairclough was getting to his knees, until the Duke put one very shiny booted foot upon his back and forced him down saying, "I collect you were attempting to abduct Mrs. Mainwaring. I suggest you go home to your Mama and forget all about it. Neither she nor anyone else will hear of it from me unless you persist in these fruitless attempts to fix the attentions of a woman who does not want you. If you do, I shall make sure your foolishness is known to everyone. London may not be very comfortable then. Good afternoon."

As he was moving back through the bushes with Imogen, he stopped. "By the way, let me know what you want for your chestnut. Apparently you were prepared to abandon it. Any price will do. You can leave a note for me at Brooke's."

With that, he led Imogen to his phaeton. Since it was a high-perch, he had to lift her bodily up to the platform. As he did this, he held her at eye level momentarily and looked at her. They could both feel her heart beating fiercely. "That's a very pretty bonnet," he said, and kissed her lightly before lifting her up the rest of the way.

The members of the *ton* walking in the park on one of the last fine days of autumn were later able to report to an amazed audience that they had seen a woman sitting up beside the Duke of Sarisbury in his phaeton, a thing he was known never to do.

When they reported that it was the widow Mainwaring, looking, however, very unlike a widow in a charming green bonnet, they were even more amazed.

"But he doesn't even know her!" was the most frequent comment. "At least, he's never sought her out at any gathering, or paid her any particular attention."

Come to think of it," someone remarked, "he hasn't been paying particular attention to any female of late. Most unlike him."

Thus, the gossip which Imogen had sought so hard to avoid was for a while rampant. But, like all rumors in London, it was a nine days' wonder, and when Mrs. Mainwaring failed to appear at any public event at which his Grace was present, the chatter soon died down.

Chapter Fifteen

After being left face-down in the park, Lord Fairclough scrambled at length to his feet and, looking around in fear that someone might have observed his discomfiture, proceeded to push cautiously through the bushes back to his curricle. His chestnut was still peacefully cropping the grass. The Duke and Imogen were nowhere to be seen. He brushed himself off as best he could and drove home, his thoughts a welter of loathing towards the Duke, disappointment in Imogen that she had allowed herself to be carried off and self-righteous indignation about the way he had been treated.

"And he had the gall to offer to buy my chestnut!" he said to himself through gritted teeth, vowing that he would not let the horse go at any price.

Walking in the front door and trying to avoid the eye of the Fairclough butler who had known him since he was a child and tended to treat him as if he were still one, he went towards the stairs, to go up to his bedchamber to change out of his muddied trousers and jacket. Unfortunately, on the bottom step, he met his mother coming down.

"Ah! Desmond!" she said, appearing at first not to notice his disheveled appearance, "Come into the drawing room. I have something I want to say to you." Then, perceiving the state of his clothing, "What on earth have you been doing with yourself? Did you fall off your horse? You are a silly boy!"

Coming on top of the Duke's treating him like a schoolboy, his mother's attributing this childish behavior to him was more than he could stand.

"Of course not, Mama," he replied hotly. "Nothing of the sort. I'm not a child! If you must know, I had a… a disagreement with the Duke of Sarisbury."

"Good gracious! A disagreement with the Duke of…," began his mother in amazement, then realizing that the servants in the hall must be agog to hear more, "come into the drawing room at once."

"I would rather go upstairs and…," he began.

"Do as you are bid!" said his mother. "I wish to have words with you and you obviously have some explaining to do."

Since he was, in fact, not much more than a boy, and since he had been taught from infancy to respect and obey his mother, he unwillingly obeyed her command and followed her into the drawing room.

"Before you explain to me how this… disagreement came about," began his lordship's mother at once, "I have something to tell you. Sit down."

"I would rather stan…."

"SIT DOWN!" repeated his mother. "Here on this old chair. I've given instructions for it to be recovered, so the disgraceful condition of your clothing doesn't matter. I can't imagine how anyone has allowed the upholstery to be reduced to this state. The dogs have been sleeping in it, no doubt."

Thus instructed, he sat, not unlike the spaniels who, as his mother had rightly surmised, generally used that chair.

"I went today to see Mrs. Mainwaring." The young lord started up and tried to remonstrate. "NO! let me finish. As I say, I went to see Mrs. Mainwaring to persuade her to... to release you from any engagement you may have made." He started up again, but his mother held up an admonishing hand and continued. "However, she assured me that she only allowed your attentions because you talked of doing injury to yourself, that she had no intention of marrying you, and in fact, her affections are engaged elsewhere. Those were her exact words: *my affections are engaged elsewhere*. Now, what have you to say to that?"

Lord Fairclough sank back into the chair. On the instant, he had nothing to say. The scales had fallen from his eyes.

"So that's why she struggled so much!" he finally muttered.

"What do you mean, struggled?"

"When I tried to get her into the coach."

"Why were you trying to get her into a coach?"

"To take her to Gretna Green, of course. We had talked about it."

"Do you mean she had agreed to go?"

"N... no, not exactly, but I thought she would."

"Do you mean you attempted to force Mrs. Mainwaring into eloping with you to Gretna Green?"

"Mama! When you put it like that, it sounds barbarous! It wasn't! I love... loved her!"

"And I presume the Duke comes into it somewhere?"

"Yes! He had he damned impudence to… to interfere."

"He stopped you? In other words, he rescued her?"

"No! Well, yes, but it wasn't like that! It wasn't a question of rescue! We were in love! Or so I thought. And all along she was in love with someone else! I was never so deceived! And on top of that, Sarisbury wants to buy my chestnut! I despise the man!"

"If your father were alive, this would kill him!" pronounced the matron. "To think that a son of ours would force an unwilling woman to elope with him! You have done some very silly things in your life, Desmond, such as when you fell in love with one of the downstairs maids and sent her pressed flowers in the shape of a heart! Don't think I've forgotten it! Or when you decided your housemaster's wife was in love with you, when all she did was bandage up your knee after you took a fall from that tree! Don't think I've forgotten that either! But this last escapade beats them all! I have never been so ashamed of you in your life! Mrs. Mainwaring was right! You must go abroad. You will go to Greece for the winter. Edward Dawkins is leaving to take up a post there. He was a friend of your father's and I'm sure he will have no objection to your traveling with him. Perhaps you may act as his secretary and I hope he gives you a great deal to do! It's time you found out what work is, instead of mooning around writing nonsense! You will return in time for the Trinity term and finish up at Oxford in time for your coming of age. No!" as her son began to protest, "No, Desmond, there will be no discussion. We have all been too lenient with you and this is the result. I will write to Edward at once and arrange it all." She swept out of the room.

Desmond, Lord Fairclough buried his head in his hands and gave way to tears. In a matter of hours, his world had fallen apart. Far from being a published poet with a bright future and a beautiful wife, permitted to come early into his fortune as a recognized genius, he was to be nothing better than a diplomat's lackey, transcribing boring notes and carrying his bags. Then when he did come back to England it would be to spend the summer term at Oxford! Oh, it was not fair! And he was sure she would make him sell his chestnut to the Duke. He knew it was useless to argue. His mother had always been the driving force in the family. In fact, he thought his father died principally to get away from her. He had been an easy-going, dreamy fellow whose wife was constantly pushing him in directions he had no wish to go. Desmond knew exactly how he must have felt.

It may be worthwhile to report that things did not turn out as badly for Lord Fairclough as he anticipated. He found he enjoyed the role of diplomat's assistant. He discovered he had a genius, not for poetry, but for parties and balls with fantastical themes and decorations, which his embassy functions gave him ample scope to develop. His fair good looks and slightly dreamy demeanor (though this was less as he grew older) endeared him to women, both young and old, and he was a highly sought-after partner.

He did finish up at Oxford, though not with any great distinction, and came of age into his full title and fortune. He almost immediately married a well-born young woman he had met in Greece, there with her parents on a lingering tour, and since she always considered him both wonderfully talented and the finest man of her acquaintance, they were very happy during a long and fruitful married life. He never forgot Imogen, though his passion for her faded as soon as his new life began. She became a beautiful memory for him, one that he always thanked in his heart for being the inspiration behind the only poem he ever published.

The Duke of Sarisbury expected no more news of young Fairclough, but was surprised late one morning not many days after his rescue of Imogen, by his butler bringing him in Lady Fairclough's card. That lady desired a few minutes of his time. Finishing up his third cup of coffee, for he had breakfasted late after an early appointment with his fencing master, he strode into the drawing room to meet his guest.

"Please sit down, Lady Fairclough," he gestured towards a comfortable chair. "May I offer you tea or coffee, or...," his eyes smiled in a way that most women, including Imogen, it may be said, found bewitching.

"Thank you, no. I will not stay long." Lady Fairclough sat and looked around appreciatively. She knew the Duke's reputation as a rake and had somehow thought that his townhouse would be a sinister lair, dark with unlit corners. In fact, nothing could be further from the truth. The room she was in had high ceilings and tall windows swathed in ivory silk overlooking what must in spring and summer be a pleasant garden at the back of the house. The furniture was of pale or painted wood with curved legs, the elegant armchairs and sofa sturdy and wide enough to be comfortable, upholstered in straw-colored silk. A huge Aubusson rug with the palest of turquoise-green backgrounds lay upon the floor and books lay scattered on the small tables, obviously not just there for decoration, but being read. It was a delightful room, saved from being too feminine by the moody landscape paintings that hung on the pale tan walls. Lady Fairclough did not recognize the work of William Turner, a favorite of the Duke. Not many knew it, but he was an art connoisseur and collected Turner's works.

"What a very pleasant room," remarked her ladyship.

"My mother's doing," replied the Duke. "The furniture is eighteenth century French, before it descended into the rococo. She had very good taste and fortunately preferred comfort to decoration. I have seen no reason to change anything, except for adding a few paintings." He did not elaborate but waited politely for her to continue with the purpose of her visit. It was not long in coming.

"My dear Duke," she said, "I am here to thank you for intervening in the recent unfortunate episode involving my son. He is a good boy, but, as you have no doubt perceived, rather silly. You saved him from making a dreadful mistake."

"I'm happy to have been of service. I have to say, though, my thought was more for the lady in the affair. She would not have married him even had he succeeded in carrying her off. She did not desire the union. But she would have suffered a permanent blow to her reputation. On the other hand, if she had married him, she would have suffered an equal blow to her happiness."

"You are quite right. My next visit is to her, with the object of seeking her pardon. I know she did everything she could do to avoid his fixing his attentions on her, short of positive unkindness. It must have been all the more difficult for her as she informed me herself when I saw her not three days ago that her affections are engaged elsewhere."

The Duke started, but quickly controlled himself. "I confess I do not know her well," he said hastily. "Er... do you know who the object of her... affections might be?'

"No, she did not say, and naturally, I did not ask. Oh," she added, "before I forget, my son says you wish to buy his chestnut. Since he will be leaving the country for some months and will have no need of it, and since also we owe you a debt of gratitude, I wish you may take it at any sum you wish to offer."

"I should be very pleased to do so. If you would not mind waiting a few minutes, I will write a draft upon my bank."

He disappeared and a short time later returned with a sealed note. "I hope this will be satisfactory. Your son's groom may bring the horse around at any time."

After a few pleasantries and with expressions of mutual esteem, the lady left. When she arrived home and gave the draft to her son, it was found, upon breaking the seal, to be a handsome sum, more, indeed, than he had paid for the animal.

"But then, of course," pronounced her ladyship, "the Duke is a gentleman."

Chapter Sixteen

The following day, Imogen had the dubious pleasure of having the study of her prospective business broken by two visitors, the first in the morning and the second in the afternoon. Lady Fairclough arrived at about eleven, to fulfill her object of apologizing for her son's intemperate behavior and to thank her for what she had done to save him from his own folly.

"I am speaking on my son's behalf, my dear Mrs. Mainwaring, as I have forbidden him to bother you again. I have taken your advice, and Desmond is to go to Greece until the beginning of the Trinity term. An old friend of my husband is, fortunately, recently posted there and my son will accompany him. I hope that real work and serious company will cure him of his fanciful ways."

"I'm sure it will. He is a very nice young man, just a little... youthful and inclined to act before he thinks. A change of scene and working with important people who do not know him and therefore will frown at rather than forgive his excesses, will do him the world of good."

They, too, parted with expressions of mutual esteem, both mildly glad they would probably never meet again.

Her afternoon visitor was the Duke of Sarisbury. He had tried to talk himself out of coming, both because he knew Imogen did not want her aunt to know they were friends, if that's what they were, and because his mission made him feel rather foolish. Nevertheless, he had his card sent into Imogen and a few minutes later bowed as she entered the drawing room.

"Good afternoon, Your Grace," she said, forcing herself to sound calm. Not for the first time, she wished she could stop her heart beating so violently whenever she saw him. "It's always a pleasure to see you."

"Is it?" he replied without preamble, not being in the mood for pleasantries. "I rather thought the opposite was true. At least, every time I see you, you scold me for some reason or another. Except the last time, when I was once more obliged to save you from death or worse. How many times is that now? Let's see. Once, from falling off the balcony in Lausanne, once from breaking your neck down the bell tower steps, once from an ugly mob of defrauded investors, and once from the grips of a villainous abductor. That's four times I've saved you, not that I've received a word of thanks, mark you."

"The only time you have actually saved me was the last one. The others were occasions when you took advantage of the situation to put your arms around me and then claim it was for safety reasons. And I think I did thank you the first time, but afterwards I realized it was just opportunism. So, thank you for saving me from the villainous abductor, though, you realize, I could easily have escaped when we stopped to change the horses. So after all, only very little thanks are required."

"Upon my word, Imogen, it's a good thing you were not born in the Middle Ages, when damsels were required to be saved by knights in shining armor. There would be no dashing tales of derring-do at all, if it were up to you."

"Quite so. As I have always told you, a woman does not need a man. Sometimes it's nice to have one, to fetch you a lemonade at a ball, or hail a hackney, or shelter you with his person from mud thrown up by carriage wheels, but other than that…. Anyway," she ended, "why are you here? What do you want?"

"My dearest love, though I deplore your unmannerly interrogation of my, as always, pure motives for seeking out your company, I want the answer to a simple question."

"I am not your dearest love, and what is the question?

"Who is the lucky man who, it is reported, has engaged your affections?"

"What are you talking about?"

"Lady Fairclough told me you said your affections were engaged elsewhere than by her dratted son."

Imogen laughed. "I only said that to convince her I wasn't looking for marriage with him. There's no one. My affections are not engaged. Why? Anyway, what do you care?"

"I care very much indeed," replied the Duke with a smile in his eye that belied the seriousness in his heart. "After all, I have been trying to engage your affections for almost a year now, with a marked lack of success. I just wondered who the paragon might be who has succeeded where I have failed."

"Well, you need wonder no more. If the day arrives when I do find someone, you will be the first to know. Now, go away before my aunt comes home. Luckily, she's out this afternoon and therefore I don't have to present you to her and hear all her strictures about not allowing men of loose morals to pollute our home."

The Duke laughed heartily. "Is that what I'm doing? Polluting your home? Indeed, I had better be off then. Goodbye, Imogen. No, don't bother to ring for the butler. I'll see my own way out." He took her hand and, turning it over, kissed her palm, as he had done before. "Don't hesitate to call on me if you need saving again." He went out of the room, chuckling, "Pollute our home!"

Imogen returned to her study, also laughing to herself and then sighing. Every time she saw Ivo Rutherford she found herself more drawn to him. He made her laugh and raised her spirits. But it was impossible. And why had he come, in fact? Was it really to find out if she had another love interest? If so, why? Could he be jealous? He had offered her his "protection" more than once, but he must know by now she would never agree to it. Surely he did not think she would change her mind? She shook her head again and bent back to her task.

Mr. Carter had told her it would need an Act of Parliament for the construction of a new rail line, because it involved the compulsory purchase of wayleave. She was now assembling facts and figures for a company prospectus to persuade a Member of Parliament from the constituency concerned to propose it. She had met with the engineer William Cubbitt, who was the acknowledged expert in the field. They had studied the route and agreed that, apart from purchasing the land over which it would run, the difficulties would lie in bridging the Medway River near its mouth and building a long tunnel under the Shakespeare Cliff near Dover. They also agreed that a somewhat circular route, which did indeed follow the old roads, as Imogen had envisaged, and by which Dover would be approached from the west, would enable the rail to be laid over easier ground than directly across the Weald. Accordingly, she wrote a prospectus with as much detail as was known and had five hundred copies printed.

For Dover, the two Members were a Whig, Charles Poulett Thomson, and a Tory, Sir John Rae Reid. Having decided that the proposal would probably be better received coming from a man, she had asked Mr. Carter to send them both the company prospectus, with an invitation to meet for discussion. If one or the other agreed to sponsor the Bill, there would be a reading in the house, then a general debate. It would probably have to go before a special committee for scrutiny of the details and after the committee's report, finally a vote. This could take several weeks, if not months. Given the disastrous speculation caused by the Farah affair, she wanted the whole proposal to be absolutely transparent, with nothing that was not completely above board and open. But she was anxious to move as quickly as possible, hopefully to have it through both Houses before the General election to be held just after the first of the year. After that, releasing shares on the Stock Exchange to raise capital could take several months and the construction would probably take up to another two to four years. In other words, this was a venture that could take years to come to completion, but Imogen was confident that it could and would be done.

Looking up at the portrait of Fordyce on her study wall, she said, "Well, my dear, what do you think?" She imagined he smiled and nodded.

In the event, The Tory Member was hesitant, after the Farah debacle, so she met only with the Whig. Mr. Carter had indicated that the Company was being formed by one I. Mainwaring, he was shocked when this turned out to be a woman. However, the force of her arguments was undeniable, and the fact that she was risking her own money was persuasive. In the end, Charles Thompson agreed to propose a Bill for the formation of the railway company. Since he was a member of the majority party, this was the most likely to result in success, and Imogen was both relieved and delighted.

In the months before and after their trip to Deal, Adrian Brody had been finishing works for an exhibition in which he had been invited to participate. This was sponsored by the Royal Academy. Mr. Brody confided in Imogen that he was sure he had been chosen because he was known to be on the fringes of the *ton*, welcomed at Almack's and on good terms with the Patronesses. The wealthy and titled would come out of interest, since they knew his name.

Imogen accompanied the artist himself to the opening night, where he was greeted by polite applause as he entered. There were three artists involved in the exhibition: Samuel Drummond, who specialized in portraits and marine genre painting, James Ward, a painter of animals and also an engraver, and Adrian himself. It was a well-chosen ensemble, as each was distinctive both in subject matter and in style. James Ward was the best known, and had in 1823 earned the fabulous sum of 500 guineas for his work entitled *Deer Stealer*. It was not for sale, but Mr. Levett, who had commissioned and paid for it, allowed it to be shown. It depicted a late evening woodland scene of a quite well-dressed man, about to use a horse to carry off a deer he has evidently shot with the gun he is carrying. The deer is bleeding, or already dead. When Imogen saw it, she found it vaguely disgusting, and wondered why it should have commanded such a price. Drummond's works also included two or three that were in private hands, alongside those for sale. Apparently, this was common practice, since it demonstrated that the artist was already collected and encouraged other buyers. They bore cards marked *PC*, which Adrian explained stood *for Private Collection*. One was a portrait of the poet Byron, whom Imogen had never met. This showed a man with a sensual, full-lipped mouth and dark brooding eyes. She had heard how attractive he was, and how women had fallen at his feet. She did not find him so, though one might have guessed he was a poet. Drummond's marine paintings were not of ships, as she had expected, but of historic scenes, notably, several views of the death of Admiral Nelson. Imogen far preferred Adrian's landscapes, and told him so.

"It's kind of you to say, me darlin'," he smiled. "And it's glad I am that I'm holding my own in the sales department."

Sure enough, three of his oils already sported discreet cards marked *Sold,* and Imogen could see groups of obviously interested parties clustered around others. Imogen quickly purchased two paintings: one of the exterior of Walmer Castle outside Deal, and one of the *Invicta* locomotive at Whitstable. Both were clearly recognizable, but had an otherworldly quality. The diffused light falling on both subjects, especially on the steam engine, made them look almost unreal and ephemeral. Adrian explained that since Fordyce's death, he had been influenced by the fleeting nature of things, even solid buildings and iron machines. In the end, he said, everything must pass, and that is what he hoped to show in his work.

Once five of his paintings displayed *Sold* cards, there was practically a rush for the others. This was helped by the charm of the artist himself, who took the time to explain what he had told Imogen, and whose bright blue eyes shone with such sincerity that the women, in particular, were immediately won over. Imogen wandered around the works of the other two painters, comparing them unfavorably with Adrian's. Although it could be argued that his work dealt with death, it was with an oblique subtlety. His paintings could also be taken simply at face value as beautiful, atmospheric views. The other two artists also dealt with death, but with a blunt, almost shocking verisimilitude. The dying deer, the wounded Nelson, were studies of death in all its reality, down to the last button or trembling hoof.

"Not for me," thought Imogen.

Then, as she rounded the last corner, she caught sight of the Duke of Sarisbury. Why was he there? she wondered. Was he interested in art? It was true that when they had looked around the historic places in Lausanne, he had seemed to know all about whatever they were looking at, but she had presumed it was from a familiarity gained over the years rather than a real interest. She walked up to him.

"I didn't expect to see you here," she said, baldly.

"Good afternoon, Mrs. Mainwaring." The Duke bowed. "As direct as ever, I see! Is it too much to hope that you're glad to see me?"

"Between old friends, is there a need for conventional formulae?" she spoke more tartly than she meant to.

"None whatsoever," he responded calmly, "if by that you mean we are old friends. I might have categorized us as old antagonists, but I suppose the two are much the same."

"Oh, don't let's bicker. I am glad to see you, in fact. I was going to write you a note, but this is quicker. May I come to talk to you about something one morning soon?"

"That depends. Is it something to my advantage? Have you decided to let me kiss you after all?" His eyes twinkled.

"Don't look at me like that. No, it isn't, though perhaps it might be, and I haven't."

"Your speech is unusually elliptical, but I collect that whatever the proposed meeting is for, is not necessarily to my advantage, though it may possibly be, and I may not kiss you. So why should I see you? I will again be left bereft, and since I'm that already, I see no future in it."

"Stop it Ivo!" she said, half laughing. "Be serious!"

"I am always serious." He smiled at her. "Oh, very well. But if you wish our friendship, or whatever it is, to remain unremarked, we'd better not continue talking like this. I will see you tomorrow afternoon. I am not generally available for visiting in the mornings." In fact, Ivo always went to a fencing academy in the mornings, but Imogen, of course, interpreted his remark as meaning he was recovering from his night-time exertions "But I shall come to you. It's best for you not to be seen entering alone the polluted house of debauchery." He bowed and walked away.

Imogen shook her head and laughed to herself. She went off to make her goodbyes to Adrian Brody, and saw him engaged in close conversation with an older, good-looking, grey-haired gentleman. As they smiled at each other, she realized that her friend had found a replacement for Fordyce and was glad for him.

"Imogen," he said as she drew near, "I want you to meet my friend Randolph West. I've told him all about you."

Mr. West bowed over her hand and said he was glad to make her acquaintance at last.

"I also wanted to ask you if it would inconvenience you greatly if I go South for the winter. I don't want to abandon you, darlin', if you think you'll have need of me, but in all truth, I need a holiday. Randolph here is suggesting the South of France, now things have settled down over there."

"I think that's an excellent idea! You've been working too hard, as all these paintings prove. And it looks as if you'll need more! Come back with canvasses full of sunshine and everyone will want them here in grey old London!"

He smiled. "I don't know if paintings of sunshine will suit me, but I feel I'm at a new beginning, sure I do." He looked up at Randolph then back at her. "But I'll not forget you, me darlin' Imogen! You'll see me back soon enough. I don't doubt you'll have a network of railways across the country by then. Tell you what, I'll paint them all and we'll hang up copies in the stations so people can see where to go next." Mr. Brody was joking, but his idea was adopted over the next ten years and his depictions of locomotives emerging like huge iron angels from clouds of steam became the face of the new industry, along with those of Joseph Turner.

The streets of London were crowded as Imogen's carriage drove home. It was a few weeks before Christmas and families were out and about, looking in the windows of the shops and, more especially, at the stalls set out by tradesmen on the sides of the roads. Seeing the children jumping up and down with excitement, or pulling a parent from stall to stall, made her conscious of a lack in her own life. She would never have a child, she thought. When she had married Fordyce, that had been the last thing on her mind. She had felt loved and wanted. The lack of physical intimacy had not troubled her. Now though, she often felt that she was missing something. Were her business concerns to be her husband, her family, her children? Was that what she wanted? She shook her head and resolved not to think about it anymore. Anyway, she was too busy.

Chapter Seventeen

Imogen's reason for wanting to talk to the Duke was entirely business-related. The Whig member had agreed to propose a Private member's Bill, but she would like the support of the Tories too, if possible. Most newspaper reports seemed to think that the General Election would return an increased Whig majority under Lord Grey, as the effects of the Reform Act eliminating the Rotten Boroughs would be felt. However, she would like the Bill passed before the Election, and support from the Tories would help. The Duke of Sarisbury was, of course, a member of the House of Lords and no doubt had Tory friends. Perhaps he was one himself; she should ask him. If he were prepared to support her, perhaps his friends would, too. This is why she wanted to speak to him.

He arrived in the middle of the following afternoon, by which time Imogen had had time to change her mind and wish she had never asked to see him. She hated asking anyone for favors. In spite of his remarks about advantages to himself, she somehow knew that Ivo would never make her do something she did not want in return for a favor, but she did not even like to give him the opportunity. She almost told the butler to say she had the headache and could not see him, but such cowardly behavior was not in her nature, so when he was shown into the drawing room, she rose to greet him with every appearance of pleasure.

"Your Grace, thank you for coming," she said.

"If you're going to 'Your Grace' me all afternoon, I shall turn around go back the way I came," he replied, before bowing to kiss her hand. "Call me Ivo or I leave."

"Don't be so difficult!" she cried. "I want to talk business with you and it's already hard enough. I thought it best to keep it on a formal footing."

"It will be on no footing at all if you don't call me by my name. I refuse to call a woman I've seen in her nightgown with her hair down 'Mrs. Mainwaring' when I'm alone with her."

"Oh, why do you bring up that dreadful occasion! I've tried to forget it! Anyway, I wasn't in my nightgown!"

"Well, I cannot and do not want to forget it. You were utterly desirable, nightgown or not, and you broke my heart. That vision of you features in my dreams." His eyes danced.

"Oh, sit down, you dreadful man! I knew it was a mistake asking you here!" She sat down herself and tried to collect her thoughts. Finally, she said in desperation, "Would you like a cup of tea?"

"Good God! No, I would not! Is that why you've invited me here? Please tell me it isn't. I don't think I can bear another disappointment."

"Of course not!" She took a breath. "The reason why I wanted to talk to you is I'm having a Bill introduced in Parliament for the formation of a Company called the Southeastern Railway Company. I wish to run a railway line to Dover, and possibly to

Canterbury and elsewhere. I'd like to get the Bill through before the General Election. I wonder whether you would be prepared to... to give it your support. You probably know a lot of the men there and they might listen to you. I can give you a copy of the prospectus. It outlines the engineering proposal and estimated costs and revenues. I've had a meeting with Charles Thompson, the Whig Member of Parliament for Dover and he has agreed to propose a Private member's Bill. I'm hoping you might speak to Sir John Reed, the Tory. He was more hesitant. It will be a long-term investment but in return for your help, I'm prepared to give you shares in the company. I have put in an initial capital of twenty-five thousand pounds and intend to reserve a portion of the shares myself. I think they will be worth a great deal one day."

"Imogen, I've said it before and I'll say it again," exclaimed the Duke, sitting back. "You amaze me! Here I am thinking you need my help to get you out of another scrape, when in fact you are proposing the formation of a railway company! When is that pretty head of yours ever at rest?" He laughed. "I'm sorry I can't use my well-known strength and derring-do to rescue you, but I'd be happy to pass along the good word. I know Johnny Reed quite well. We were at Eton together. But you know, I can't accept any gift of shares from you, even if I wanted to, which I don't, because that would be bribery, my love. I will help you because it seems a good idea to me and because I wish you well." He paused and his eyes twinkled wickedly. "On the other hand, if you want to repay me, I can think of something else...."

"Ivo!" Imogen interrupted him ruthlessly. "Don't even say it! The answer will still be no!"

"I was only going to say that I would be happy with a kiss! Just a kiss! Is that too much to ask? It seems a minor payment for such a favor." He stood up and walked over to her, pulled her to her feet and into his arms. Before she could say anything, he kissed her, his tongue feeling gently between her lips. Then his embrace became harder. He held her closer and pushed his tongue into her mouth. His hand cupped her breast. Her heart was thumping so hard he must have been able to feel it. After a few moments, he broke away.

"Damn it!" he said half laughing, striding over to the other side of the room, his back towards her. "I'd better stop now before I do something I regret."

He took a deep breath, and then another, obviously forcing himself to calm down. Finally, he turned to look at her. "Yes, I will do as you ask. Have your man send me the prospectus. But you'd better not invite me here again unless your aunt is to be in the room. Good afternoon, Imogen. I hope your plans all come to fruition. I'll see myself out."

He bowed, went quickly to the door and was gone before she had a chance to say a word.

Imogen sat for a long time, her hands in her lap, staring into space. Her heart gradually returned to its normal rhythm, but still she sat. She knew that some sort of threshold had been stepped over. She could no longer pretend that Ivo Rutherford was just a friend, that his kisses were simply playful or teasing. Like him, she had felt herself on the verge of doing something she would regret. The power of her feelings had almost overwhelmed her, just as on that day on the lake.

But she could not run away, as she had from Lausanne. Her whole life was her business and business was in London. She would simply have to avoid his company from now on, even if it meant going to no more balls, no parties, no Almack's. The prospect did not really alarm her. She was finally forced to admit to herself that more than half the reason she had gone to these things anyway was to see him. She had little interest in them for their own sake. She had her books and her newspapers, for now she subscribed to all the newspapers in the country, which even though they arrived later than *The Times*, often supplied the background to stories she had read there. She would not allow herself to think about what she might be missing. She would focus entirely on the development of her business.

She was not surprised, for she knew the Duke to be a man of his word, when a week or so later she saw a report in *The Times*.

> *A Private Member's Bill for the development of a railway line to Dover was today put before the House by Charles Poullett Thompson, supported by Sir John Rae Reed, both Members for Dover. In light of the Farah affair, which we reported on several months ago, in which investors were the victims of an unscrupulous fraud, this new proposal occasioned a good deal of debate.*

> *The Duke of Sarisbury spoke at length and with conviction in support of the Bill. He said that the nationwide spread of the railways was inevitable. Their time had come and nothing would stop them. This new line, with the goal of making the port of Dover easily accessible from London, would be built, if not today, then tomorrow, but it would be built. If Britain were to retain her place as the industrial leader of Europe let it rather be today than tomorrow. Let the honorable Peers, his colleagues, take the lead in pushing the way towards a country united not only in spirit but in rapid and reliable*

communication between its great centers and its ports.

He further said that the principals involved in the formation of the company proposing were personally known to him and he had every confidence in their careful, honest management. He proposed to invest in the company himself as soon as shares became available.

The Bill passed the first vote. It now moves to Committee, with a report expected before the end of the year. With support from both sides of the House, the chances of a rapid passage look positive.

Imogen smiled at the image of the Duke speaking at *length and with conviction*, and thought that she herself would undoubtedly have been persuaded by his smiling eyes and silver tongue.

Once the examination of the Bill was underway, Imogen felt it was time for her to prepare to list her new company on the London Stock Exchange. Mr. Carter advised her to have a well-known bank such as Rothschilds manage the Stock Exchange offering, so an appointment was made with that august establishment. The bank Directors were astonished to see a woman enter the room, since Mr. Carter had again referred to her simply as I. Mainwaring. But once she had reviewed the company prospectus and the financial benefits she envisaged, their business interests overcame their distrust of her sex. They agreed to manage the offering and set the share price. After a discussion between the bankers, an offering of twenty-five thousand shares at a guinea a share was suggested. Imogen, knowing nothing about how such things were valued, agreed, simply saying she wished to retain an additional twenty-five thousand shares herself and instructing Mr. Carter to free up assets to that amount. Next she went with Mr. Carter to the Capel Court building that had been expressly constructed for the Stock Exchange some thirty years before. The Registrar, who first addressed himself to Mr. Carter, was as astonished as the Rothschilds Directors to learn that hers was the principal name on the paperwork. It was she who registered The South Eastern and Dover Railway Company and her initial investment. Then all she had to do was wait.

She held to her vow not to go anywhere she might encounter the Duke. She had explained to her aunt that at present her business was taking all her attention. She was sorry not to be able to accompany her to any evening entertainments. Her aunt, well believing this to be the truth, was either happy to stay at home herself, where she had small card parties with her most intimate friends, or go occasionally to Almack's. Since she was familiar with the place by now, she did not feel averse to going there with only her companion by her side. Lady Jersey always greeted her with a friendly smile and asked after Imogen. Upon being told that she was too occupied with business to attend, that lady frowned a little and urged Aunt Dorothea to tell Imogen not to become a too much like a man. She was far too lovely for that and there were a number of gentlemen needing pretty partners. They were all missing Adrian Brody, too. As Lady Jersey said, he could charm the birds off the trees.

It was after one such soirée that her aunt came home saying it had been a delightful evening. Everyone had asked after her; there were several new young Pinks of Fashion who entertained them all with their outlandishly styled jackets and violently colored hose, not to mention their gyrations on the dance-floor;

that redheaded woman they had seen dancing with the Duke all those weeks ago was wearing a dress so diaphanous and her petticoat so dampened that she looked practically naked; and that the Duke himself had ignored all the lures thrown out at him. He had disappeared into the card room and had not emerged until it was time to leave. Mrs. Arbuthnot, one of Aunt Dorothea's particular cronies, and an incurable gossip, had told her that the *ton* was all abuzz with the notion that the Duke was a reformed man. He had spoken in the House, a thing he had never done since his maiden speech over ten years ago, and he appeared to have deserted the petticoat company. He had not been seen with a fair Cytherean on his arm for weeks. No one could account for it. A couple of his friends had apparently asked what was going on, and he had answered with his usual nonchalance that he had no idea what they were talking about.

Imogen absorbed all this and wondered. She had not seen the Duke for some time, but she still found herself thinking about him, especially about the evening when she had asked for his support. She recalled the intense feelings his kiss had aroused in her, and also, apparently, in him. It would have been easier had she been busy, but for the first time in many months she found herself with nothing to do. All she had to do was wait.

After the excitement of the move to London and her entry into the *ton*, then the investigation into Farah and preparation of her business prospectus, the meetings with parliamentarians and her visit to the Stock Exchange, not to mention the determined courtship of Lord Fairclough, it all felt drearily flat. All the thoughts she had had during the carriage ride back from the art gallery came flooding back. Was business all she wanted out of life? She tried to concentrate on the matter in hand. She wrote notes to Mr. Carter almost daily about issues that had already been addressed, and then tore them up, realizing she was being ridiculous. She feverishly scanned all the newspapers for scraps of information she might have missed. She went to the art galleries Adrian had introduced her to, but missed his insights, and even more his company. She walked around the park and even found herself missing Lord Fairclough. That was when she knew she needed more.

The truth was that though she tried not to think about Ivo Rutherford, she thought about him all the time. He made her laugh, he annoyed her in the extreme but he brought her to life. Yes, that was it. She finally admitted to herself that when he was near, she felt more alive than at any other moment, even when she was in a room full of men talking about her business proposals. But in order to avoid him, she was spending long evenings alone, in front of the fire or retiring to her bedchamber almost immediately after dinner. Why? Why was she so determined to refuse his offer of "protection"? It had been instinctive in her to do so, but now she began to examine the situation objectively. Was the life she had now better? Since she was out of her weeds, she could present herself on the marriage market, but would she find someone else who excited her a tenth as much as the Duke? She certainly had not met anyone in the previous six months. Gentlemen had tried to engage her, but, just as in Nottingham, she had found them all so boring. Either that, or she could tell they were only interested in her fortune.

Unlike most of the women she had known, she was not interested in marriage for its own sake. She did not want a man at any price. She already had her own home and she had plenty of money. She was a grown woman in control of her own life. Couldn't she do what she liked with it? What did it matter if after a few weeks, or months, Ivo Rutherford tired of her, or she of him? So what if she were left alone again? In many ways she was alone now. Aunt Dorothea had her own life and Adrian had a new love. At least she would have *lived*! It was only convention that was dictating her present state and she had already shown she was unconventional. What did she have to lose? She thought of Lady Jersey. She certainly ignored convention. Why shouldn't Imogen Mainwaring? And then, she thought, would Fordyce really want her to deny herself a chance of happiness, even if it were fleeting? She knew he would not. She fought with herself for nearly another week, then made a decision.

One evening Aunt Dorothea was invited to an early dinner at one of her friends, before going on to a ridotto: a concert followed by a party. She had encouraged Imogen to go with her, but the prospect of dining with six or eight elderly people and then listening to a warbling soprano entirely failed to attract her. Besides, she had other plans. As soon as her aunt left, Imogen went upstairs and dressed herself in the gown she knew became her best. It was of shot silk with an alternating weave of green and amber, so that the two different colors shone as the light fell upon it. It had a low décolleté which revealed the ivory of her bosom, and it fit to perfection, revealing her curves but not excessively tight. She pulled on long lace gloves, but left off her widow's cap. She arranged her curls on the top of her head and threaded an amber ribbon through them. Amber drop earrings that Fordyce had given her on their first anniversary fell from her ears. She knew she looked her best. She went down to her study and stood in front of the portrait of her husband.

"Forgive me, my dear, for wearing these and for what I am about to do," she gestured at her earrings. "But I have to do this. I know you understand."

She put on her heavy winter cloak with a hood that covered her curls and slipped out of the front door without being observed by any of the servants. They would think she had gone up to her bedchamber early, as had been her recent habit. Outside, in the crisp winter night, she hailed a hackney and gave the Duke's address on Grosvenor Square. It was still only just after nine. Hopefully, he would have just dined and would not yet have left for his club, or whatever other amusement he had planned.

Chapter Eighteen

When the doorbell rang, the Duke was sitting in the drawing room by the fire reading, had he known it, the same newspaper that Imogen had pored over earlier that day. The light was muted, as he preferred the gaslights in the drawing room to be turned down from their full blaze and he had a candle on the table next to his chair. He had dined alone at home and a glass of port stood at his elbow. He had told Hunter, his butler, that he was not at home to anyone, so he was surprised when the man came in on silent feet and announced that he had a visitor.

"Mrs. Mainwaring is asking to see you, Your Grace." Through the unaccountable osmosis by which servants always knew everything, Hunter clearly knew who Imogen was.

"Good God!" The Duke nearly knocked over his port. "Show her in! Don't leave her standing in the hall!"

Presently, Imogen was ushered through the door. Hunter had taken her cloak, and she stood in the lowered gaslight, the firelight making her curls glow, her bosom rising and falling in obvious agitation.

Standing up, the Duke gestured to his man, "Thank you Hunter, that will be all." Then, turning to his visitor, "Imogen! What in God's name are you doing here?" He took her by the arm and led her to the chair opposite his by the fire. She was trembling, but not from the cold. They both sat.

It had only been by the exercise of absolute will-power that she had rung the doorbell. The closer she got to Grosvenor Square, the more she had felt like telling the hack to turn around. But here she was. She forced herself to stop trembling and to act normally. She looked around. Her reaction to his Grace's pleasant drawing room was the same as Lady Fairclough's. It was quite unlike what she had expected. The light colors of the walls and furniture reflected the warm glow of the fire and in the lowered gaslight, the room was cozy, inviting.

"What a nice room!" she exclaimed, glad for something to say that did not immediately answer Ivo's question. "Are those Adrian's paintings?" She gestured at the walls on either side of the fireplace, where, indeed, two of the first three of Adrian's sold paintings were hanging. "So it was you who bought them! Why?"

"Because I liked them, of course! Why else? I have collected art for some years. But I don't imagine you're here to critique my collection. Suppose you tell me why you *are* here."

"I... I wanted to talk to you," Imogen found it difficult to start. Then, squaring her shoulders, she looked straight at him. "First of all, thank you for supporting my Bill in the House of Lords. I read about your speech in The Times. It was very fine." The Duke started to respond, but Imogen held up her hand. "No, please, Ivo, don't. It's hard for me to say what I have to say, so I'd better come out with it all at once, before I lose my courage." She took a deep breath, "Since the Bill has gone into Committee and I'm not so busy, not busy at all, in fact, I've had a lot of time to think. And I realize that apart from my business interests, my life is empty. I'm not really living, I'm just existing." She held up her hand again, as Ivo began to speak. "No, please let me finish." She gave him a rueful smile. "Perhaps you haven't noticed, but I've been avoiding you these last weeks." The Duke began to speak again, but she hurried on, "And by not seeing you, I realized I'd lost one of the things most important to me. The only person who has made me really alive is you. You enrage me, you make me laugh, I dislike you and I love you, all at once. I don't want to see you and I can't bear it when I don't. I think of you all the time. No one else makes me feel this way, and no one ever has. So," she hesitated again, but then plunged on, "so, I've come to ask you if your offer is still open. Your *carte blanche*? If you still want me, I accept. I know it will only be temporary, and you will tire of me sooner or later, but I've decided I prefer a temporary full life to a permanent half one."

There was a moment's silence during which the Duke was, for once, speechless.

Then Imogen carried hurriedly on. "There is one thing, though, that I have to tell you." She hesitated again, looking down at her gloved hands. "The thing is… you see… from hints you've given occasionally, I'm sure you know my husband Fordyce was… well, he was not like most other men. He loved me but he didn't love me… as a man normally would." She looked up into his eyes. "He didn't deceive me. He told me before we were married he wasn't interested in the… the physical side of marriage. So, we never… we never…," she sought desperately for words. "The marriage was never consummated. I'm still, I'm still…."

"A virgin," concluded his Grace, with a sigh, then shook his head. "God in heaven, Imogen, why didn't you tell me?"

She laughed shakily, "Tell you, Ivo? When? How? What moment is right for such a declaration?"

"When I kept trying to get you into my bed! You must have known I thought you were... experienced. I told you I'm not in the business of seducing maidens."

"I know you told me that, but I didn't think... I...."

"So the answer," interrupted the Duke, not letting her finish, "the answer, my dear, is no. The offer of a *carte blanche* is not still open to you."

It was Imogen's turn to be struck speechless. Then, her eyes filling with tears, she exclaimed, "But what am I to do, Ivo? How can I gain experience if you won't have me and you're the only man I want?"

"You marry me," replied his Grace calmly. "It seems quite obvious."

"M... *marry* you? But you've said repeatedly you're not the marrying kind. I don't want you to marry me out of pity!" Tears began to roll down her cheeks. "Oh, why am I crying? I never cry!"

The Duke silently reached inside his jacket, pulled out a handkerchief and handed it across to her. "I'm not asking you out of pity, you goose, except pity for myself that it's taken this long. Good God, Imogen! I've been trying to fix your affections for nearly a year but instead of sharing this vital piece of information with me, you've been constantly running away, repulsing me, calling me dreadful and ridiculous, saying the only person you need protection from is me, that you don't need a man except to bring you lemonade and...."

Imogen stood up, dropped the handkerchief and ran over to where he was sitting. He had got out of his chair when she did, and she stood on tiptoe, flinging her arms around his neck. "But that was because I loved you, only I didn't know it! I've never been in love before!"

She pulled his head down so that she could press her lips to his. Then, uncertainly, she touched the tip of her tongue to his. He groaned, and sat down, pulling her onto his lap. His tongue thrust into her mouth and his hand found her breast. She felt her nipples harden instantly and, as he not so gently pinched her there, she pulled away from his mouth with a gasp. He pulled her back into the kiss and pinched her again.

"If you're going to kiss me in that low-cut gown," growled the Duke, when he finally let her go, "you'd better get used to more than a little pinch."

"I was just surprised, that's all, I wasn't expecting it. No one's ever touched me like that before." she replied, her head on his shoulder. "But Ivo!" she looked up urgently, "Did you *really* ask me to marry you, or did I dream it?"

"I didn't ask you, I just said it was obvious you should. But I will ask you if you like. Do you want me to go down on one knee?"

"Yes, please. Then I'll know it's real."

"Very well. Stand up."

Imogen scrambled off his knee and stood up. She found the dropped handkerchief and scrubbed her damp cheeks. The Duke also stood, then knelt on one knee and, looking up into her eyes, took her hand.

"Imogen Mainwaring, will you do me the honor of becoming my wife?"

"Yes, Ivo Rutherford, I will," she replied, looking back into his eyes. "With all my heart."

"Then you make me the happiest of men." The Duke stood up and, putting one arm around her waist, lifted her up to his eye level. "The first thing I am going to do is find a stool for you to stand on so I can kiss you without bending in half. For the time being, we'll have to manage like this."

He kissed her, not at all gently, and this time, when his free hand found her breast, she relaxed and enjoyed it. But suddenly, an inescapable question occurred to her. She put her hands flat on his chest, pushed him away and slid her feet to the floor.

"But Ivo!" she said, "I've just thought: you will be faithful to me, won't you? I don't think I could bear it if you had other women. I'm sorry, but I can't be one of those complaisant wives who turn a blind eye. I'd rather not marry you at all if that's how it would be. I'd rather be your mistress, after all. If you don't think you can change your ways, I'll just go and have an affair with someone else, I don't care who, so that then you can give me a *carte blanche*. How about that?"

"Setting aside that I'm affronted you should be doing all this thinking while I'm kissing you, no, you may not go and have an affair with someone else, because then I should have to kill him, deliberately this time, and be forced to leave the country again. Look at me, Imogen." He lifted her chin and looked her in the eyes. "I give you my word of honor that I will be faithful to you. I love you. You will be my wife and my love as long as we both shall live."

Tears came to her eyes again, but neither of them could find the handkerchief.

"If you're going to cry every time I say I love you, I won't say it again!" Ivo laughed. "I haven't enough handkerchiefs! Come and sit down again."

After a few very pleasant minutes, he stood her up from his lap and went to pull the bell.

"Champagne, if you please, Hunter," he said when the butler appeared, "and you may wish us joy."

"I do wish you joy, Sir, you and Mrs. Mainwaring. And I know the rest of the staff will do likewise." He bowed and left, returning in a few minutes with a bottle and two glasses, which he set carefully on a table.

"You may pour and then leave the bottle. Go down and open a few bottles for yourself and the rest of the staff. The good stuff, mind. I don't want you drinking our health with anything inferior."

After serving them, Hunter bowed his thanks and went down to find the whole household already collected, agog to hear more. The butler had briefly told them the news when he had come down for the champagne. Mingled with their joy for him, since the Duke was a good and popular employer, there was general amazement. They were well accustomed to his libertine propensities and the endless procession of women through the house, and never thought this day would come.

"But what's she doing coming here alone at this time of night?" enquired the cook, a woman of middle years, permanently grumpy at being required to assist the volatile French chef who presided over the kitchen, but too fond of her generous wage to seek employment elsewhere, "I'll not doubt she's no better than she should be."

"Now, now, Mrs. Walker," interjected Hunter. "No need to be talking like that. Mrs. Mainwaring is a most ladylike person, very pretty behaved but not at all high. The Duke would never make himself tenant for life with any lightskirt, and you should know it!"

"Well, that's true enough," accepted that lady "but when you think of some of them that's been here!"

And they collectively launched into reminiscences of some of their employer's more extreme ladyloves, the stories becoming more and more lurid as the champagne flowed. A couple of the youngest maids were obliged, unwillingly, to leave the room. Though far from the only memorable visitors, amongst them stood out the one who descended the main staircase by riding down the bannister, arriving in a heap at the bottom, her skirts over her head, revealing she had neither petticoat nor chemise, or the one who was discovered in the dining room wearing nothing but lemon slices or the one who arrived in a heavy black veil and cloak, only to reveal that under it all she was naked as a jaybird. They were at last called to order by Hunter who asked them to raise their glasses in a toast, which, with exceeding good will, they did.

Meanwhile, in the drawing room, his Grace had returned to his armchair with his lady on his knee, since this was the only position that brought their heads to anywhere near the same height, and was plying her with a second glass of champagne.

"No, Ivo, you know I can't!" Imogen cried, "Remember Lake Lausanne!"

"I do remember it, and as I told you then," he replied, refilling her glass, "it was not the champagne that made you dizzy."

"How silly I was!" she sipped reflectively at her glass. "But it was just as well, because if it hadn't turned out the way it did, I would never have become interested in business and be where I am today, just about to launch my very own company."

"Why not? You don't think I would have stopped you, do you? No, my dear, you are as free to pursue your own career as you like, and become as rich as Croesus into the bargain, provided you don't prefer reading *The Times* to going to bed with me."

She looked up at him. "Can we do that tonight... go to bed I mean? I had quite made up my mind to do that when I came."

Ivo gave a great sigh. "No, dammit, we cannot. I cannot believe I'm saying this, but a virgin you are and a virgin you will remain till our wedding night." Imogen began to protest and he laughed. "I'm sorry to disappoint you. I promise I won't do so when the time comes. But it's a matter of honor."

"Oh!" said Imogen, not knowing whether to be pleased or disappointed.

He shook his head ruefully, "I feel like crying myself. Since your speech about the eventual sorry outcome for women who live under a man's protection, I've been living the life of a monk all these weeks. Not that you were there to notice, of course. But I tell you, Imogen, I'm not waiting more than another two weeks. You go to your *modiste* tomorrow and tell her I'll pay her any amount she names to have your wedding clothes ready in a fortnight. I'll see to the arrangements for the Abbey, put the notice in the newspapers and everything else."

He set her on her feet. "Now you must go home. I'll call tomorrow afternoon and we can give your aunt the good news. You'd better have smelling salts handy. She'll probably have an apoplexy."

He stood up and rang the bell again. It was some time before the butler appeared and it was clear he had taken his Grace at his word concerning the champagne.

"If you can stop carousing a moment, Hunter, call the carriage to take Mrs. Mainwaring home. I will accompany her."

"But I can take a hack, Ivo! That's how I came. And you don't need to go all that way and come back!"

"The future Duchess of Sarisbury take a common hack? Alone? I should think not! You have to consider my position, my dear." He laughed. "What would people think?"

"You know you couldn't care less what people think," she smiled back at him.

"Very true, but I do care about the woman I love travelling alone across London at night, leaving a house of debauchery in the carriage belonging to a well-known rake."

Chapter Nineteen

On the following day, his Grace's secretary caused the following notice to appear in all the London newspapers:

The House of Sarisbury is pleased to announce the forthcoming nuptials of his Grace Ivo Hillier Rutherford, fourth Duke of Sarisbury, to Imogen Margaret Mainwaring, née Edwards, widow of Fordyce Giles Mainwaring, to be celebrated at Westminster Abbey on the nineteenth of December at three o'clock in the afternoon.

The news exploded on the *ton* like a bomb. The women who had been the object of his favors and who still carried a hope in their hearts, either left town to avoid witnessing the dashing of their dreams, or vowed never again to acknowledge by so much as a glance either of them. Many of the town beaux rejoiced at a deliverance that would leave the playing field much clearer, while others, confirmed bachelors, shook their head in sorrow over the loss of such a *game 'un*.

Aunt Dorothea did indeed need the smelling salts when the news was broken to her. Imogen decided it was kinder to tell her in advance of Ivo's arrival, so she would have time to collect her wits.

"But my dear," she wailed, "you don't even know him! I don't believe you've so much as spoken to him! How can you marry him? Do you owe him a great deal of money? If so, all I have is at your disposal to pay him off!"

When Imogen laughingly denied she owed the Duke anything, her aunt persevered. "Then is it because I have been leaving you alone so much in the evenings? I declare I shall never stir out of doors again if you will but tell me it's all a mistake!"

"No, no, Aunt! I do know him. I met him in Switzerland back in March. I have spoken to him many times, just... just in secret, you know, as I was sure you would disapprove."

"I *do* disapprove, Imogen! What your poor mother and father would say, I can't conceive! And your cousin! How can I ever tell him that you came to live with me and ended up marrying a rake? A man with the worst reputation in London! And Fordyce! What would he think?"

"Rightly speaking, Aunt, *you* came to live with *me*, and I don't give a fig what my cousin thinks. And I am certain Fordyce would be happy for me. I am marrying Ivo Rutherford and there's an end to it. I don't care what his reputation is. I love him and I believe he loves me. Let there be no more discussion. He is coming here this afternoon to make your acquaintance, but if you cannot meet him with dignity, then I shall tell him not to come."

She spoke with such assurance and dignity herself, that at last her aunt agreed to see his Grace, though she said if she tried to say anything welcoming to him, her tongue would cleave to the roof of her mouth.

"Then say nothing, Aunt. Just nod and try not to look so disapproving!"

In the event, Ivo's visit passed off better than anyone might have expected. Not for nothing was he renowned for the persuasiveness of his address, especially with women. Determined at first to be aloof and unfriendly, Aunt Dorothea soon melted under the influence of those smiling eyes and excellent manners. He treated her as a contemporary and gently flirted with her, until she felt like a girl again. After his departure, Aunt Dorothea declared herself very satisfied with the Duke.

"Indeed," she said, "I feel that those who criticize him cannot know him. Or their jealousy causes them to exaggerate. He is clearly a man of culture and breeding. I shall be delighted to welcome him into the family. I shall write to Nottingham and tell them so."

When Imogen reported this to Ivo, he remarked that he had always told her his motives were never anything but the purest and his reputation entirely undeserved. Since he accompanied this by a twinkle and a loving pat on the bottom, she just laughed. The following day, the Duke drove Imogen to a small, unremarkable shop in the City. It proved to be the jewelers who had served the Rutherford family for generations.

"We must have the wedding ring cleaned and sized," he explained. "My mother was much taller than you and it's most likely too big as it is. It came originally from my great-great grandmother and was probably tiny then. It has been added to and subtracted from with every new Duchess. I hope you don't mind, but the wives of the Duke have worn it forever."

Imogen hardly knew how to reply. The ring was a heavy, wide, old gold affair with the letter S deeply engraved upon it. She was beginning to realize what it would mean to be the Duchess and to have the weight of family tradition behind her.

"I am honored to wear the same ring as the previous Duchesses," she said seriously, and meant it.

His Grace appeared as calm and unconcerned as ever, but all around him, people were furiously making the myriad arrangements required for a wedding that promised to be the society event of the year, to take place in two weeks. His housekeeper was tasked with organizing a dinner for forty at Sarisbury House, followed by a ball for two hundred. His secretary made the arrangements at the Abbey, where, they all agreed, anyone who wanted could attend. But when it came to invitations to the dinner, they spent a frustrating afternoon poring over lists of who had to be invited and who they would like to invite. Imogen had a very small family and Ivo only one aged infirm uncle, but the list of possible invitees seemed equivalent to a state occasion. Once again, Imogen had a glimpse of what her new responsibilities would be.

She found herself frantically busy. She made several visits to her *modiste,* who was delighted to be making the wedding gown and other wedding clothes for the future Duchess and willingly pushed all her other clients to one side. Imogen also needed to decide which of her possessions she wished to move to Sarisbury house. It was difficult to give up Fordyce's furniture, but she had to admit that the Duke's residence was furnished in beautiful taste, so in the end, she decided to take only the paintings by Adrian Brody and the portraits of Fordyce and herself. The Duke had offered her a large salon on the ground floor as her study, laughing that her commercial interests needed space to expand, so the first thing she did was to transfer the portraits there.

Another task that fell to her was making arrangements for housing her cousin and his family in London for several days before and after the wedding, since the Capital was almost entirely unknown to them. She wanted to rent a house for them and have Mr. Carter find temporary servants, but her aunt exclaimed that she would love to have her little great nieces with her, and to have the opportunity for long chats with her nephew's wife, so Imogen reluctantly gave in. It turned out as she knew it would. She was left to deal with the little girls most of the time, as they tired her aunt, their mother was too indolent, and the nanny was too fearful even to leave the house, fearing footpads and pickpockets even in the adjacent park. They would cling to Cousin Imogen's skirts, begging to go out with her, and she generally obliged, finding them easier to deal with outside than in.

She took them to the Pantheon Bazaar, which they found the most exciting place imaginable, chiefly because it had fallen even further down the social scale and now housed a number of enterprises selling all sorts of animals. It was only by exercising the firmest of vetoes that she was able to leave there without a kitten and a monkey, both of which the girls found essential to their future happiness. She took them to see Stephenson's Rocket, the steam locomotive, built some ten years earlier and now overtaken by more modern designs. She found it fascinating, but the little girls saw nothing of interest in what they considered a pile of metal on wheels and begged to go back go see the dear little kittens and the naughty monkey at the Bazaar.

Not much better than the children was her cousin who would waylay her and engage her in long conversations about her business enterprises. Since he was not a man of flexible intellect, this usually ending up with his shaking his head and advising her to have nothing to do with these newfangled ideas, which were sure to end in ruin. She avoided telling him that she was in fact, proposing to put a large sum of money into a new company to exploit the newfangled idea, and was just waiting for the release of the shares on the Stock Market.

It was, therefore, with enormous relief that she met daily with the Duke, most often for dinner and most often at Sarisbury House, as his Grace's French chef was determined to show the future Duchess the perfection of his dishes. But this too was fraught, since it was a time of frustration for both of them, as Imogen repeated her desire to stay the night, and the Duke, masking his increasing discomfort with a smile, refused.

"Please, my love," he said finally, "don't mention it again! It's more than flesh and bone can bear to deny you. For the only time in my life I have a beautiful woman begging me to take her to my bed and I have to say no. I tell you, I am going to commission that statue of myself I talked about in Lausanne and have it titled *Forbearance*. It will become required study for all young men of virtue!"

Though the face he showed to the outside world continued as ever to be calm and smiling, the one place his Grace's frustration was all too visible was at his fencing sessions in the mornings. He became more and more fiercely aggressive until only the master would practice with him. And he stayed longer than was strictly necessary under the cold-water hose, the only form of ablution provided by the establishment for the hot and perspiring practitioners.

At last, the day of the wedding arrived, cold and clear, just six days before Christmas. The wedding was at three in the afternoon. Dinner guests would be received at Sarisbury House at seven and the ball would begin at ten. The Duke saw no reason to cancel his fencing session and spent a satisfactory couple of hours enjoying his last fight as a single man, a fact he celebrated by distributing a number of very fine cigars and a case of champagne. He then walked home in a good mood, ate a hearty breakfast, and took a leisurely bath. He strolled over to his club where he suffered the good-natured chaffing of his cronies, ate a late lunch, and distributed more cigars. He played a few hands of cards and finally wandered home in time for his valet to dress him.

His knee-length, black superfine waisted jacket, cut away in front, fit with such perfection that there was not a shadow of a wrinkle across his broad shoulders. His pale grey trousers were perfectly slim and straight down to his polished shoes. His waistcoat, which fit close, with lapels revealed by the cutaway jacket, was of a small black and grey check. The starched white collar of his shirt stood up to just below his chin, and a neckcloth, carefully folded by the Duke himself, lay in swathed perfection around his neck, held with a diamond pin. A new top hat, gold-topped cane and grey kid gloves completed the ensemble. He looked magnificent. Even his valet, who was accustomed to his master's sartorial elegance, drew in his breath. He knew that his place in the pantheon of gentlemen's gentlemen was assured by today's work.

Imogen, on the other hand, had had a fitful night, excited and anxious as all brides must be, and had only fallen into a refreshing sleep three or four hours before she was woken up by the maid with a cup of tea. She would have liked to go back to sleep, but her plans were shattered by the precipitate arrival of the two young ladies who wanted her to settle an argument about the strewing of rose petals before her path into the Abbey. They would be silk, since real roses were unavailable in that season. She had reluctantly agreed they could do this, because their

Mama was so taken with the pretty picture they would make, and now they were having a heated discussion about the procedure.

"Mary says we should go one at a time, with her in front of me," complained Lucy, the younger sibling. "But that's not fair!"

"But I'm the oldest, so it *is* fair," retorted Mary, "Anyway, she'll probably just throw all the petals in one clump, because she doesn't know *how!*"

"I do, so, know how!" cried Lucy, near to tears. "Just because I'm younger doesn't mean I can't do things, does it, Cousin Imogen?"

"Girls, girls," shushed Imogen, "you can both do them at the same time, one on the right, one on the left. Just be sure to keep the petals *down*. Don't throw them up into people's eyes!"

Thereupon, the two girls paraded around the room in their nightgowns, throwing imaginary rose petals from imaginary baskets with greater and greater abandon until one succeeded in knocking the other on the head, with resulting screams, accusations, and tears.

"That's *enough*!" cried Imogen, with unwonted asperity. "Go away now and leave me in peace, for heaven's sake!" Then, a little acidly, "Go and see if Mama is awake and tell her what we decided."

She had scarcely settled down when a tap came at her door, followed by the figure of her aunt. This good lady came in tiptoeing, as she saw it, but as she was never exactly light on her feet, and of considerable girth, this was more like the movement of a battleship coming into port.

"Oh, good, you're awake, my dear," she said, giving her niece a kiss on the cheek, "I woke up thinking about the carriages."

Imogen sighed. This had been the object of innumerable discussions already. The Duke had insisted on sending the most official-looking coach in his stable to convey her to the Abbey. It was a huge affair, emblazoned on both sides with the Sarisbury crest, drawn by four matched black horses, complete with plumes, liveried driver, grooms, and postilions. After the service, the same coach would convey the married couple back to Sarisbury House. The Duke himself would be brought to the Abbey by his old friend the Earl of Wendover, in that gentleman's carriage.

"I think it unreasonable, after all, for you to be conveyed in that huge coach all by yourself, while the five of us crush into your own much smaller carriage," said her aunt. "The servants and others will come in my old bone-rattler, of course, but I am persuaded that your cousin should ride with you. As your nearest relative, he will walk you down the aisle, after all."

This had been the subject of much debate. Her cousin's wife had pronounced herself unable to travel anywhere or go anywhere without her husband by her side. Her nerves would not stand it, she said. Imogen had privately thought it was because she never wanted to do a thing herself, and without her husband she would have to deal with both the children and the aunt. Imogen had, in any case, said she was perfectly prepared to walk herself down the aisle, and the husband and wife could go together. But now this was about to be changed again.

"But I thought this all decided, Aunt! Emily finds herself unable to face anything without Henry. Don't let's change it now." She felt she could not deal with any more disputes before breakfast. "But," she had a brainwave. "If you are afraid of being crushed, why don't you ride with me? That would solve everyone's problem."

"I?" said her aunt, wonderingly. "Ride with you in the Sarisbury coach? Why! That would indeed solve the problem." She did not say that this was just the solution she would have proposed herself, had she dared. She was a kind old woman who as a general rule did not push herself forward, but, like most people, was always ready to be treated royally if the opportunity arose. "I shall tell Emily presently."

The result of this was that when Imogen, who decided that sleep was no longer an option, arrived dressed at the breakfast table, she found a heated discussion in progress.

"My dear!" said her cousin's wife. "If I had thought that a female companion was acceptable to you to ride in your coach, I would have proposed myself! I am sure it is better sprung than yours, and, as you know, I am particularly susceptible to rough roads!"

Imogen did know. She had been treated to a long description of Emily's woes when she first arrived. That lady declared herself so prostrated by the trip from Nottingham that she did not even think she would be restored in time for the wedding.

"I don't think you will find the roads between here and the Abbey very rough, Emily," replied Imogen, "and, anyway, I thought you were nervous to go anywhere without Henry by your side."

"Oh, now I am more familiar with the place, I think I shall be able to manage," came the airy reply.

But for once, Imogen was not to fall in with her cousin's wishes. "Anyway, it is all decided. My aunt shall ride with me. We have been good companions these last six months and it is fitting she be my companion this one last time."

She spoke with unusual firmness and even Emily could see it was no use arguing. She said no more, though her demeanor as she left the table was far from gracious.

Wanting nothing more than a little peace after breakfast, Imogen went into her study and closed the door. She tried reading the newspapers but the words swam before her eyes. After a while, she gave in, put her head down on her desk and closed her eyes. But no sooner had she done so than she was awoken by a knock. The butler brought in a note.

"This has just arrived for you, Madam. It appears to be urgent"

Indeed, the envelope had the words *Urgent Deliver At Once* inscribed on the outside. Imogen recognized the handwriting of Mr. Carter. Shaking the sleep from her eyes, she tore it open and read:

> *Dear Mrs. Mainwaring,*
>
> *I am most reluctant to disturb you, today of all days, and would not do so were the matter not of extreme importance.*
>
> *It seems that there remains one document requiring your signature that was somehow overlooked when we completed the signings at the Stock Exchange. The signature must be witnessed by Exchange officials, otherwise I would have brought the document to you. I was only informed of this this morning. I do not know how it happened and I ask you to accept my deepest apologies.*
>
> *I must ask you to return there as soon as you can. Without this signature, the opening of your Company on the market cannot proceed. Since I am*

reliably informed the House will vote today on the proposed railway line, to complete outstanding business before Christmas, I'm sure you do not wish to lose even one day.

I shall be awaiting you in Capel Court.

Again, with my apologies and in haste
Martin Carter, Esq.

Imogen threw down the envelope and ran out of her study and upstairs for her hat and cloak, calling for the carriage to be brought round at once. Her cousin emerged from the drawing room and attempted to discover what the commotion could be, but she ignored him, knowing that any conversation with him and his prosy discourse would inevitably delay her. She crammed her hat on her head and strode up and down outside on the pavement, waiting for her carriage. The minute it was there, she leaped in and gave the order for Capel Court.

The crowd on the roads seemed especially bad that morning. Knife-grinders, boot-cleaners, street-sweepers, pot-menders, chimney-sweeps, holly-and-ivy-sellers, carts, carriages, coaches, curricles, barouches, landaus, single horsemen, and pedestrians, all jostled for space. The distance to the old City seemed longer than ever, and Imogen was in a fever of impatience long before she arrived. She found herself wanting to tear at her hair, but had the sudden reflection that she needed her curls in at least a semblance of order for later that day. Was she really going to be married and yet here she was on her way to the Stock Exchange? It did not seem possible.

At last she was there. Telling the coachman not to go far, she dashed into the huge open space that was the floor of the Exchange. Her sudden and no doubt farouche appearance caused all conversation to cease, but she hardly noticed. However, the sudden lull and craned necks caused Mr. Carter to look in her direction and in a moment he was by her side, ushering her into a small office. The important but innocuous-looking document, looking just like the many others she had signed, was soon produced. She trusted that Mr. Carter had read all the fine print, which he assured her he had, and Imogen signed it with relief.

"I cannot thank you enough for coming, Mrs. Mainwaring," said her man of business. "I am so sincerely sorry to have made you come all this way when you must be thinking about preparing yourself for your wedding this afternoon. I thank you, by the way, for your invitation to the dinner and ball later. My wife is gratified by your kindness, as am I, and we hope to find space in the Abbey. She is going very early and I shall meet her there."

"I'm glad you can come, Mr. Carter. You have done more than anyone to help me these last months, and I want you to know that whoever the Duke has to manage his affairs, you will continue, I hope, to manage mine."

Mr. Carter smiled and bowed. "With the very greatest of pleasure, Mrs. Mainwaring, though I shall soon have to remember to call you *Your Grace*. Let us hope this afternoon brings us good news."

He accompanied her to the door of the Exchange and handed her into her carriage. The trip back was as trying as the trip there, but Imogen was lulled by the rocking of the carriage, even with its frequent stops and starts, and managed to sleep a little before arriving home. She was hoping for a peaceful lunch and perhaps a short nap afterwards.

Chapter Twenty

It was not to be. Imogen arrived home to a scene of chaos. Mary was crying because Lucy had stepped upon the ruffle of her dress and torn the lace edge. Lucy was wailing because her sister had boxed her ears. Emily was complaining in a shrill voice that the girls were driving her mad, without, however, doing anything to settle their argument. Aunt Dorothea fell on her and sobbed that her dresser had had a moment of inattention and scorched her new bombazine. Henry loudly demanded to know where she had been and Waring, the butler, between all the babble, was trying to ask if luncheon should be served, since it was already gone noon.

Never had Imogen wished more that she were a little taller. It was hard to be commanding at five feet four inches. So she mounted the first five steps of the stairs and clapped her hands loudly.

"Be *quiet*, everyone! It's time you all gave some thought to the fact that today is *my wedding day*! Since early this morning I have been beset with quarrels and questions and I know not what. It must end, or, just to be quit of all of you, I shall leave this house now, drive to his Grace's and ask him to take me to the Abbey as I am. Unlike you, I know he would put my comfort above all other concerns."

Her listeners were stunned into silence. Imogen had never used this tone with them before and they were suddenly ashamed of their selfishness.

"Emily, please ask your maid to fix Mary's lace. Lucy, apologize to Mary and stop crying. Mary, say you're sorry for boxing your sister's ears. Aunt, tell your dresser to rub white vinegar on the scorch. Henry, for your information, I have been to the Stock Exchange to sign some papers for shares in my company that will most likely be offered today under Rothschilds' management. The shares will be valued at a guinea each. It is to build a railway to run from London to Dover. I recommend you invest in it, as I am sure it will make a lot of money. Waring, tell cook luncheon is to be served in half an hour. I am going upstairs to take off my coat and hat. I do not want a single interruption, and I expect no more quarrelling. If they can manage to control themselves, and since this is my last meal in this house as an unmarried lady, Mary and Lucy may lunch with us. That is all."

She swept up the stairs, leaving a shocked audience behind. When she came down, half an hour later, it was a subdued group that met her in the drawing room. She took her aunt on her arm and led her into the dining room, followed by her cousin and his wife and lastly the two little girls, suitably chastened. Since it was her last meal as mistress of the house, her cook had made a special effort, and the meal was delicious. In fact, the only discordant note was struck by Cousin Henry, who commented that he never ate so well at home, a remark calculated to flatter Imogen, but which succeeded in bringing a frown to his wife's face. Other than that, the meal passed pleasantly, with everyone determined to please and be pleased.

It was gone half past one when Imogen finally made it upstairs. She had to be at the Abbey at three, so she had not a moment to spare. The hoped-for nap was not to be. Weary, but nonetheless excited, she quickly undressed and bathed. Her maid, the same one who had been with her all along and remembered the Duke from Lausanne, remarked,

"Who would have thought, Madam, when we met his Grace in that funny hotel, that you would be marrying him? It's a strange world we live in, isn't it? Just to think, the next time I do your hair it will be in the Duke's home."

"It is indeed, and I still can't believe it myself," replied Imogen, suddenly assailed by the reality that all her *next times* would be in Sarisbury House; the next time she took a bath, the next time she sat in front of a dressing table, the next time she went to bed…. Her heart leaped and she had to take a deep breath to calm it.

For her wedding, Imogen had chosen a long-sleeved sage green silk gown with a white lace overdress. The gown had a low décolleté, for both she and her *modiste* knew her bosom was one of her finest features, but the overdress had a higher neckline. This provided tantalizing glimpses of her bosom beneath the lace, without being immodest for church. The overdress had a short train, as she considered herself too undersized for a long one. It would be looped onto her wrist for dancing. Her lace gloves of the same design as the overdress.

The headdress had proved a problem; since it was her second marriage, she could hardly wear a veil, and she would have liked to wear a flower crown, but this was unavailable in December. However, on one of her trips to the Pantheon Bazaar, amongst the kittens and monkeys she had found a place that still sold ribbon. There she had discovered a mossy green ribbon embroidered with white flowers. Threaded around her curls, which were piled on her head, it looked almost like a crown of flowers, and having her hair up like that made her a little taller, so she was almost satisfied.

"Oh, I do wish I were taller!" she complained. "When one is so short and squat one can never look really elegant."

"But, Madam, you are never short and squat! Your figure is in perfect proportion to your height. And you look lovely! There's one man at least who likes you just the way you are!" Her maid gave her an arch look.

"Yes, but even he says I need a stool so that he can kiss me." She broke off, realizing she had revealed an inappropriate intimacy.

"Oh, Madam, how funny! A stool!" and she went off into a peal of laughter.

Before any more could be said on the subject, Imogen realized that the clock had just struck the half-hour, and they needed to be on their way. Asking her maid to pick up a white fur cloak the Duke had insisted he buy for her, she looked around her bedchamber one last time, and opened the door. As she approached the head of the stairs, she could see the whole household waiting below for her. There were murmurs of appreciation and even a smattering of applause as she descended. When she got near the bottom, she stopped and looked at everyone.

"I want to thank you all for the help and support you have given me since I arrived in London. You have made my home here a very happy one, and I shall not forget it. My aunt will remain here, as you know, and I'm sure I shall be a frequent visitor. I have instructed Waring to serve champagne tonight at your table, and

I hope you will all drink a toast to me and my new husband, the Duke. Please enjoy yourselves and thank you again."

This time there was a loud round of applause as she walked to the front door. She took the fur cloak from her maid, and Waring helped her put it on. He then bowed over her hand with murmured thanks. The huge coach was waiting outside, with grooms either side of the crested doors. They bowed as she approached. Her cousin handed her up, then his aunt. The grooms drew the stools from under the seats for the ladies' feet, since all the Duke's carriages were built for someone well over six feet tall, closed the doors and gave the signal. They were off.

There was a huge crowd outside the Abbey and a collective "Ahh!" as the coach pulled up. The grooms put down the steps and helped her aunt descend, but Imogen remained where she was, to give the others in the carriages behind her time to enter and be seated. Then her cousin helped her down. Applause and murmurs of appreciation ran through the crowd. The little girls went before her, carefully scattering rose petals exactly as they had been told, and the great organ struck up with the *Trumpet Voluntary*, composed over a hundred years before, filling the august space with a wonderful sound of acclamation.

The congregation stood as Imogen walked down the aisle on her cousin's arm, arriving at last in front of the altar, where Ivo Rutherford, Duke of Sarisbury, stood waiting. Necks were craned as people, especially the women, sought a better view. Amongst them were not a few who had harbored their own thwarted expectations in respect of the Duke, but even they, jealous as they were, had to reluctantly admit that this virtually unknown Mrs. Mainwaring was a lovely bride. Ivo turned, gave her a loving smile, took her hand, and bowed over it. She stood next to him and the service began.

From the pronouncement of the first words, *Dearly Beloved*, through the moment which surely every bride dreads, when the congregation is asked if they know of any impediment to the marriage, and the recital of the vows, Imogen felt as if she were in another world. When Ivo placed the ring on her finger, with the words she knew were coming, *With this ring I thee wed, with my body I thee worship and with all my worldly goods I thee endow*, her knees began to shake, and it was as well that they were then required to kneel for the blessing and the ringing commendation *Those whom God hath joined together, let no man put asunder.*

The choir sang the soaring *Jesu, Joy of Man's Desiring.* The minister gave a sermon and read passages from the Bible, which Imogen knew well, since she had been to a number of weddings, but of which she heard not one word. Finally, to the glorious sound of the choir singing the *Ode to Joy*, they proceeded side by side back down the aisle and left the Abbey as man and wife.

The bells pealed, the people cheered, and the smiling Duke led his bride firmly through the throng to his coach. Inside Imogen found her cloak, which she had left there, and Ivo his coat, put there by his valet. He put it on, turned and putting his hand in his pockets, drew out handfuls of small silver coins, which he threw into the crowd. Handful after handful he threw, until nearly everyone was involved with picking up coins and hardly noticed when the coach drew away.

They both sank thankfully onto the squabs, and Ivo reached under the seat for the stool for Imogen's feet. They smiled at each other.

"Oh, Ivo," said Imogen, "it was a wonderful wedding! The flowers were lovely and the music was beautiful, but I'm so glad it's over!"

"I know what you mean," replied her husband. "I think we should do it again in a few months, when the pressure is off."

"Did your heart stop when he asked if anyone knew an impediment? Mine did."

"Why?" He grinned at her. "I warned all my other wives to keep their mouths shut."

"Oh, you...." She slid down the bench and put her arms around his neck. "If they come around, I'll fight them all off. You're mine!"

"Yes, I am. And you're mine. You're wearing the ring to prove it. Oh, that reminds me." He put his hand inside his coat and drew out a small box. "As a rule, one gives an engagement ring before the wedding, but it took several days to have it made. I'm sorry for the delay, my love, but here it is."

Imogen opened the box and found herself looking at a ring with a large square cut emerald surrounded by diamonds.

"I bought the stone months ago, since the minute I saw it, I thought of you." said her husband. "The green is just the color of your eyes. But as you were still rebuffing me at every turn, I never had an occasion to have the ring made. You would probably have thrown it in my face! Here, let me put it on your finger. It should fit; I had it sized from the wedding ring."

He slipped the ring on top of the Sarisbury wedding band. It fit perfectly. Imogen stared at it on her hand, speechless. Fordyce had bought her emeralds because of her eyes, but this stone was perfect. The stone was of a clear, transparent saturated green with just a hint of blue and the diamonds caught the last of the winter light.

"Oh...," she sighed. "It's absolutely lovely! *Thank you*, Ivo. It's the most beautiful emerald I've ever seen!"

She placed her left hand on top of his, wiggling her fingers in the dying light.

"Look how well it matches my wedding gown! It's perfect!"

"It does match very well, but I have to say, I'm looking forward to seeing it when there's no gown to match it at all!" He raised his eyebrows at her, "which I hope will be in less than an hour from now."

Though she had, of course, often thought of her wedding night, with a mixture of longing and anxiety, Imogen had been so busy for so long that she had given no thought to what would happen at Sarisbury House in the two hours before the first guests arrived. Now she realized what his Grace was expecting and blushed.

"Don't tell me you are suddenly maidenly!" chuckled her husband. "You've been trying to seduce me for two weeks!"

"I know, but now it's real and... oh, Ivo! I hope I don't disappoint you!"

"Impossible!" The Duke gathered her into his arms. "You cannot possibly disappoint me, and, without any false modestly, I may say I'm quite sure I won't disappoint you!" He laughed and kissed her hand. "Don't worry about it, my love. You will find it all comes quite naturally."

She tried to laugh with him, but her heart was in her throat.

When they arrived at Sarisbury House, it was to find the whole staff lined up in the hall to greet their new Duchess. Imogen had already met the butler, the housekeeper, the chef, and the cook, since she had been involved in the arrangements for the dinner and ball. But as the large number of other individuals bowed and curtseyed, she wondered how long it would be before she knew all their names. She was also astonished it took so many people to look after one person, well, two now, and said as much to the Duke.

"Is it a lot? I've never thought about it," he replied. "I just carried on with what my mother had. I couldn't just let them go for no reason. This is their home too. Do you think I should?"

"Of course not," said Imogen, "you're quite right."

"Good Lord! Don't tell me you're already an obedient wife, agreeing with everything I say. I don't believe it!" He led her towards the stairs, telling Hunter they would ring when anything was required, and said in a low voice, "But since you're being so agreeable, I'd like you to go to your room and remove your gown. I'll be with you very shortly."

He led her to the bedchamber traditionally used by the Duchess and opened the door. The housekeeper had shown her the room, unused since the time of the last duchess, but, for propriety's sake, she had never been there with the Duke. It was a large, high-ceilinged chamber, now glowing in the firelight, decorated in the same style as the drawing room, but very feminine, with light walls, and a large Aubusson rug in shades of pale rose and gold. The bed and window hangings were in the lightest of pink silk. The matrimonial bed had a fanciful wrought gold metal headboard, but no footboard. The housekeeper had told her the Duke had recently had it removed to allow for his height.

A door communicated with his Grace's room, which Imogen had never seen. Ivo lit the candles in a branched chandelier on the dressing table, kissed her lightly and disappeared into his room. Imogen tried to undo her gown, but she could not reach the small buttons all down the back. Her maid had done them up, and she needed help. Suddenly very weary, she sat down on the bed and wondered if she should pull the bell. She had not seen her own maid downstairs and did not know if she had arrived yet. The fire was warm, the candlelight soft and she was too tired to think clearly. She lay down on her side and put her head on the pillow. In thirty seconds, she was fast asleep. When the Duke came in ten minutes later, wearing only his shirt and trousers, wanting nothing so much as to make love to Imogen at last, he saw the love of his life asleep, her feet dangling towards the floor and her head on the pillow. He tenderly removed her shoes and put her feet up, covered her with the silk bedspread, kissed her gently on the cheek and left her to sleep.

Chapter Twenty-one

An hour later, downstairs was abuzz with dinner preparations. The huge table had been laid for forty, branched chandeliers down the center, alternating with epergnes of fruit from the Sarisbury hothouses. Gleaming silver chargers and cutlery with the Sarisbury crest engraved on each piece lay at each place, together with crystal glasses. The napery was gleaming white, and in the glow of the two huge fireplaces, the whole room shone, even before the candles were lit. Since it was a wedding dinner, the host and hostess would sit side by side at the head of the table. Imogen had been afraid at first that she would be at one end and her husband at the other: she would need opera glasses to see him!

Imogen slept on, blissfully unaware of the ticking of the clock. At last, when guests were no more than an hour from arriving, Ivo summoned her maid, who was by now downstairs, and sent her to rouse her mistress with a cup of tea. Shaken gently awake, Imogen eventually came out of her deep slumber and was immediately assailed by panic. What time was it? Where was Ivo? How could she have slept at such a time? Her gown was crumpled, her ribbon crown was knocked crookedly to one side of her head and her face was creased from lying on a folded sheet. In a wild start she leaped from the bed and stood in her stockinged feet, in a dither of indecision. Luckily, her maid was a practical Nottingham girl who had grown up in a large family where everything was always in chaos, and it took more than this to shake her composure.

"Have no fear, Madam... or, I should say, Your Grace," she soothed. "I'll just take your dress downstairs and give it a quick press. The lace overdress hasn't creased badly, and it will cover any problems with the silk underneath. The irons are already on the hearth, as I guessed how it would be when his Grace said you'd fallen asleep in your wedding gown. Do you just wash your face and brush out your hair. I'll be back in a shake to do it up again." She undid all the buttons that had thwarted Imogen, and then helped her take off her gown and her petticoat.

She left the room just ahead of his Grace coming in through the communicating door. He beheld his beloved standing indecisively in the middle of the room in her fine cotton chemise, through which her curves were distinctly visible in the candlelight, her curls half up and half down, the green ribbon in a tangle amongst them, still more than half asleep. She looked utterly desirable.

"Oh, Ivo! I'm so sorry!" she ran to him. "I couldn't undo my buttons and I sat down for a minute and...."

"You fell asleep," muttered her husband holding her through the thin fabric of her chemise, barely able to control the surge of desire that ran though him. Then, collecting himself, "Come, sit down, let me brush your hair."

He made no mention of her state of undress, though he could hardly concentrate on anything else.

When the maid came back, she found her lady sitting at the dressing table in her flimsy chemise, with his Grace carefully brushing thorough her tangled curls. She was a sensible girl, and this view of her mistress very much *en déshabillé* with her new husband did not shock her. She did, however, dismiss him politely but firmly, saying there was no time to waste. It was the first time a maidservant had spoken to him so decisively since he was a boy. He wondered how this plain-spoken young woman would get on with his valet, himself a proponent of speaking without preamble, and decided he was looking forward to their inevitable skirmishes.

So it was that when the guests, many of them representing the highest echelons of society, and others from the ranks of government ministers, including the Prime Minister himself, began to arrive, the Duke and Duchess of Sarisbury were in the hall, ready to receive them. Amongst this august assembly, Imogen was very happy to greet her aunt and her companion, her cousin and his wife, and Mr. Carter with his spouse. She held out her hands to greet them, and was at first taken aback when the gentlemen bowed very formally and the ladies gave her a low curtsey. She had expected it from strangers, but not from her family and friends, and once again, felt all the weight of her position.

After his deep bow, Mr. Carter approached her and said softly, "I know this is neither the time nor the place, but I feel I must tell you that your Bill passed in both houses today with a large majority. The shares were immediately released and, according to my sources, are being snapped up. Congratulations, Your Grace!"

Imogen shook his hand most warmly and thanked him, then, overcome by other events, promptly forgot all about it.

The dinner was excellent, fresh meat and produce having been brought up in carriage-loads from the Sarisbury estate. One surprise was that, as well as the almond tarts, mince pies and apple turnovers Imogen and the housekeeper had planned, dessert also included lemon creams.

"My wife told me some time ago that this was her favorite," commented his Grace, squeezing her hand, "though she claimed she would not eat them every day. I cannot understand why. There are some things that one deserves to indulge in very regularly."

Imogen looked down at her plate and blushed, but by this time the guests had so enjoyed the wines and were mostly so red in the face themselves, that no one noticed.

There were the speeches one always expects on such occasions, some humorous, some admonishing, each ending with a toast, for which the guests were well supplied with wine. Imogen drank little alcohol at the best of times, and found the array of different wines with each course quite overwhelming. The gentlemen guests appeared to enjoy it all very much, however, with remarks like "My God! Is this the Yquem that your father put down in 1811? I've heard about it but never had the chance to taste it before. They say it's the vintage of the century!" and "This can't be the 1798 Château Lafite? I didn't know anyone in London had any. I heard it all went to the Dutch!" She wondered how they could drink one glass of each, let alone the several they seemed to enjoy, and then be able to get up from the table. At last, however, hearing the clock strike quarter past nine, and knowing the Ball was to begin at ten, she stood up from the table. Her husband immediately rose, as did the rest of the gentlemen, and the ladies left them to their port.

Several of the bedrooms had been made available for the ladies to refresh themselves, with the housekeeper and maids at hand to help them. Imogen was followed to her bedchamber by her aunt and her cousin's wife, the first overawed by the grandeur of it all and the second doing her best to act as if an invitation to dine with aristocracy and government ministers was an everyday occurrence. By the time she had dealt with them, Imogen barely had ten minutes to tuck up errant curls, check her gown and wash her hands before she heard the clock strike quarter to the hour and she knew she would have to make her way to the ballroom. This took up the whole of one side of the house on the ground floor. She hoped Ivo would not have been kept so long at the after-dinner session with the gentlemen that she would be alone there, but just as she had this uncomfortable thought, he came in from his room, caught her up in a kiss and said, "Well, Your Grace, are you ready to meet your public?" and led her downstairs.

The presentation of the huge number of guests seemed endless, especially as Imogen knew few of them well, and some not at all.

Lady Jersey greeted her in her usual free style, "So, when your aunt told me you were busy with your business, we now see that that business was! Snagging the most sought-after man in London! Well done! And as for you, Duke," she said, addressing his Grace, "you are a dark horse, and no mistake! Too late for me to try my luck, I suppose!" and with a loud laugh, she sailed off.

The Ball was to begin, as customary, with the Grande Promenade, in which the first pair, in this case the newlyweds, would gradually be joined in a long line by the rest of the couples. Since these were many, four lines had to be formed. At the end, it was a lovely sight: the rows of ladies in their best gowns, shimmering with jewels, many with plumes in their headdress, and the gentlemen in their swallowtail coats and white britches. After the Promenade came the country dances and the Cotillion. Then came a Minuet, which Imogen had decided to include because though it was old fashioned, it would suit the older dancers with its ceremony and grace. Interspersed with these were the waltzes, now perfectly commonplace in London ballrooms. The Ball would end with the good old Sir Roger de Coverley.

Guests would then be served a supper, laid out as a buffet in the dining room, with the traditional white soup followed by various delicious *amuse-bouches* created by the excited French chef, who saw this as an opportunity to dazzle all the *ton*. Diners could eat anywhere they could find a seat. Imogen had not been able to prevent Ivo from scrawling his name on her dance-card next to all the waltzes. In truth, Imogen did not want to dance them with anyone else, but normally it was not considered seemly to dance more than twice with the same man, even one's husband.

"I'm damned if I'm letting any other man put his arm around you on our wedding night," her husband retorted. "If other people don't like it, they can leave. In fact, I wish they would."

For Imogen, waltzing with Ivo was a dream. She had never done it before, having been careful not to allow their friendship to become generally known. She knew they were an ill-assorted pair, he so tall and she barely average height, and she thought with some bitterness of the sight of Ivo with the willowy redhead. But from the time he put his large, warm hand on her back and led her irresistibly around the room, smiling down at her, she was lost. She felt such a yearning for him that at the end of the first waltz she was in a daze and hardly knew what she was doing. The second was even worse. Afterwards, she had no idea how she had managed to complete the steps. She had no memory of it. His Grace must have felt the same for, when the last chords of the music died away, he kept his hand on her back and urged her, not towards one of the gold spindle-legged chairs that stood around the ballroom, but towards the door. Passing through, he had a quiet word with Hunter, who stood there like a sentry, then continued to urge her firmly towards the stairs.

"What are you doing?" she asked in an urgent whisper. "Where are we going?"

"Upstairs. That's it. I've waited long enough!"

"But the guests... my dance card... we can't just leave our own Ball!"

"We can and we shall. Hunter will look after it."

He pushed her inexorably in front of him and up the wide staircase. After the first two or three steps she turned and faced him. A couple of steps higher than he, her face was level with his.

"But really Ivo! We *can't*!"

"But really Imogen! We *can*. We are. We will. I. Don't. Care."

With every declaration he kissed her on the lips and pushed her, backwards, one step further up the stairs. At last, she gave in, turned around and walked quickly up the remaining steps. As soon as they were at the top and around the bend out of view, her took her and kissed her properly, his tongue urgently probing her mouth, and his hand on her breast. They were both panting when they reached her bedchamber.

"Turn around," said his Grace without preamble. "I don't want you falling asleep again."

With a practiced hand he undid all the tiny buttons and slipped her gown over her shoulders. Then he undid the ribbons of her petticoat, which followed the gown to the carpet. When she made to pick them up, he growled, "Leave them. Take off your shoes and stockings. You may keep on your chemise." His tone admitted no discussion.

He pulled off his jacket, ripped off his neckcloth then bent to remove his own shoes and stockings. He pulled his shirt over his head without undoing the buttons, which Imogen could hear pinging into the corners of the room, and turned to pick her up and toss her bodily onto the bed.

"Wait, Ivo! The coverlet! Let me turn it down! It's so pretty!" cried Imogen.

"Damn the coverlet!" retorted his Grace.

But as he looked down to unbutton his britches, Imogen pushed the pale pink silk bedcover to the foot of the bed, where it fell in a heap on top of the gown, shoes, stockings, coat, shirt and presently britches that were tossed there.

Later, his Grace's voice came muffled as he lay face down on the pillow, his chest heaving.

"Well, what do you think? Better than lemon cream?"

Imogen sighed with satisfaction. "Oh, much, much better! And you're right. I *do* want it every day!" She turned and gently stroked his broad back. "Perhaps even more than once?"

"Good God, woman, give me a chance!" said the Duke, turning over and looking at her.

"I didn't mean right away!" she said guiltily, "unless... unless you want to."

"Of course I *want* to, my dear, but it's not as simple as that. I have to wait for the butler to refill my glass, so to speak."

Imogen thought this over, then suddenly, clutching the sheet to cover her breasts, her curls all a-tumble, the green ribbon once more crazily askew, she sat up and said excitedly, "I forgot to tell you! Mr. Carter says my Bill passed and the shares were offered this afternoon on the Stock Exchange. He says they're doing very well. Isn't that wonderful?"

"Not nearly as wonderful as the sight of you naked in bed next to me at last," said Ivo Rutherford, Duke of Sarisbury. He turned towards her, pulling down the sheet she was holding. "I think the butler just refilled the glass, by the way. Hang the Stock Exchange!"

The End

A Note from the Author

If you enjoyed this novel, please leave a review! Go to the Amazon page or use the code below and scroll down past all the other books Amazon wants you to buy(!) till you get to the review click.

https://www.amazon.com/Imogen-Love-Money-Historical-Romance/dp/1706786913/ref=tmm

For a free short story and to listen to me read the first chapter of all my Regencies, please go to the website:

https://romancenovelsbyglrobinson.com

Thank you!

Regency Novels by GL Robinson

My Amazon Author Pages: GLRobinson-US   GLRobinson-UK

Imogen or Love and Money Lovely young widow Imogen is pursued by Lord Ivo, a well-known rake. She angrily rejects him and concentrates on continuing her late husband's business enterprises. But will she find that money is more important than love?

Cecilia or Too Tall to Love Orphaned Cecilia, too tall and too outspoken for acceptance by the *ton,* is determined to open a school for girls in London's East End slums, but is lacking funds. When Lord Tommy Allenby offers her a way out, will she get more than she bargained for?

Rosemary or Too Clever to Love Governess Rosemary is forced to move with her pupil, the romantically-minded Marianne, to live with the girl's guardian, a strict gentleman with old fashioned ideas about young women should behave. Can she save the one from her own folly and persuade the other that she isn't just a not-so-pretty face?

The Kissing Ball A collection of Regency short stories, not just for Christmas. All sorts of seasons and reasons!

The Earl and The Mud-Covered Maiden *The House of Hale Book One*. When a handsome stranger covers her in mud driving too fast and then lies about his name, little does Sophy know her world is about to change forever.

The Earl and His Lady *The House of Hale Book Two*. Sophy and Lysander are married, but she is unused to London society and he's very proud of his family name. It's a rocky beginning for both of them.

The Earl and The Heir *The House of Hale Book Three*. The Hale family has a new heir, in the shape of Sylvester, a handful of a little boy with a lively curiosity. His mother is curious too, about her husband's past. They both get themselves in a lot of trouble.

The Lord and the Red-Headed Hornet Orphaned Amelia talks her way into a man's job as secretary to a member of the aristocracy. She's looking for a post in the Diplomatic Service for her twin brother. But he wants to join the army. And her boss goes missing on the day he is supposed to show up for a wager. Can feisty Amelia save them both?

The Lord and the Cat's Meow A love tangle between a Lord, a retired Colonel, a lovely debutante, and a fierce animal rights activist. But Horace the cat knows what he wants. He sorts it out.

The Lord and the Bluestocking The Marquess of Hastings is good-looking and rich but is a little odd. Nowadays he would probably be diagnosed as having Asperger's syndrome. To find a wife he scandalizes the ton by advertising in the newspaper. Elisabeth Maxwell is having no luck finding a publisher for her children's book and is willing to marry him to escape an overbearing step-father. This gently amusing story introduces us to an unusual but endearing Regency couple. The question is: can they possibly co-exist, let alone find happiness?

About The Author

GL Robinson is a retired French professor who took to writing Regency Romances in 2018. She dedicates all her books to her sister, who died unexpectedly that year and who, like her, had a lifelong love of the genre. She remembers the two of them reading Georgette Heyer after lights out under the covers in their convent boarding school and giggling together in delicious complicity.

Brought up in the south of England, she has spent the last forty years in upstate New York with her American husband. She likes gardening, talking with her grandchildren and sitting by the fire. She still reads Georgette Heyer.

Made in United States
Orlando, FL
23 April 2022

17124805R00145